"OH, MY!" EXCLAIMED Poppy, almost breathless.

"Am I flying poorly?" Luci asked.

"Just fine," Poppy managed. She tried to determine where she was, telling herself she would need to return home on her own. Luci, however, was going so fast it was hard to pick out landmarks. Besides, the sun was all but down. The only light was coming from the far west.

Luci dipped deeper among the tall, dark trees, darting around them with such sharp turns and shifts, Poppy became giddy. "Do you live in a tree?" she asked.

"Oh no, we live in a cave."

Even as she spoke, the young bat broke away from the trees. Flying swiftly if somewhat erratically, Luci was now heading right toward a high cliff. As far as Poppy could see, it was a wall of solid stone.

"Luci!" cried Poppy. "There's a rock cliff straight ahead! Shouldn't you turn?"

"I don't think so," said Luci, continuing to fly straight toward the face of the rock.

Poppy had no doubt the young bat was about to crash. She closed her eyes and said, "Good-bye, world!"

Praise for the Poppy books:

RAGWEED

"A crackerjack tale that's pure delight from start to finish."

—*Publishers Weekly* (starred review)

POPPY

Boston Globe–Horn Book Award Winner

SLJ Best Book

Booklist Editors' Choice

ALA Notable Book

"IRRESISTIBLE!" —*Publishers Weekly* (starred review)

POPPY AND RYE

"A sequel worthy of its predecessor." —*The Horn Book*

ERETH'S BIRTHDAY

"A must-read for fans of the series." —ALA *Booklist*

POPPY'S RETURN

"A heartwarming tale of friends, family, and home."

—*Chicago Tribune*

POPPY AND ERETH

"A satisfying conclusion to a heartfelt series."

—*The Horn Book*

AVI

Poppy and Ereth

ILLUSTRATED BY *Brian Floca*

HARPER

An Imprint of HarperCollins*Publishers*

Brian Floca wishes to thank Justine Wilbur and the Prospect Park Zoo of Brooklyn, New York, for a close look at the zoo's resident *Erethizon dorsatum*, Brody the porcupine.

Poppy and Ereth
 For information address HarperCollins Children's Books, a division of HarperCollins Publishers, 10 East 53rd Street, New York, NY 10022.

www.harpercollinschildrens.com

Library of Congress Cataloging-in-Publication Data

Avi, date.

Poppy and Ereth / Avi ; illustrated by Brian Floca. — 1st ed.

p. cm.

Summary: After a long, hard winter in Dimwood forest, Poppy the deer mouse finds new adventure thrust upon her while helping Ereth the porcupine, along with making new friends.

ISBN 978-0-06-111971-2

[1. Mice—Fiction. 2. Porcupines—Fiction. 3. Animals—Fiction. 4. Friendship—Fiction. 5. Adventure and adventurers—Fiction.]

I. Floca, Brian, ill. II. Title.

PZ7.A953Poe 2009 2008019662

[Fic]—dc22 CIP

AC

Typography by Karin Paprocki

11 12 13 14 15 CG/CW 10 9 8 7 6 5 4 3 2 1

❖

First paperback edition, 2011

For Brian Floca

Dear Friends of Poppy:

It has been quite a while since I first began to write the Poppy stories.

Truly, when I started, I did not think Poppy's story would go on for as long as it has, or create a cast of characters for whom I have developed so much affection. Each time I have come back to them, it has been like a joyous family reunion. For, sometimes, a writer is lucky: he invents characters who allow continual discovery, who keep surprises coming, who keep growing.

In your hands is *Poppy and Ereth*, the last book in the series. While wanting to bring the Poppy saga to a satisfying end, I have worked hard to join many of the characters, events, and memories of the previous five books. My desire is to evoke the past even as the future unfolds.

It is my fondest hope that you—as I already have—will gather this final tale to your heart as much as you have taken to the others.

Avi

Contents

TO LONG LAKE

TO THE FOX DEN

CORN FIELD

OLD BARN

TO THE WOODLANDS AND BEAVER POND

DIMWOOD FORES

ENTRANCE TO THE BAT CAVE

BOUNDER'S CAVE

TO AMPERVILLE

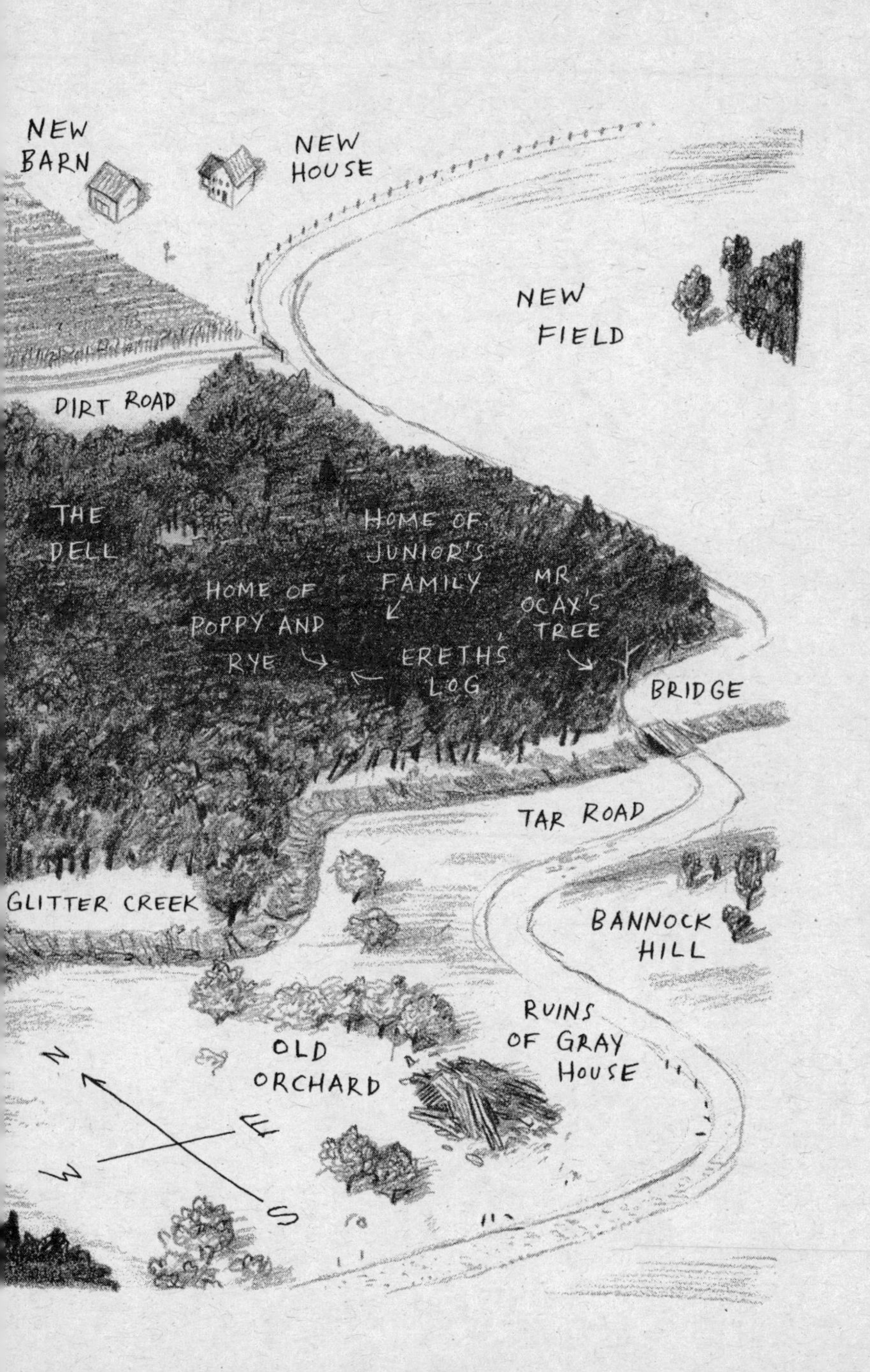
NEW BARN
NEW HOUSE
NEW FIELD
DIRT ROAD
THE DELL
HOME OF JUNIOR'S FAMILY
HOME OF POPPY AND RYE
MR. OCAX'S TREE
ERETH'S LOG
BRIDGE
TAR ROAD
GLITTER CREEK
BANNOCK HILL
RUINS OF GRAY HOUSE
OLD ORCHARD
N
E
W
S

CHAPTER I

The Hard Winter

IT WAS A HARD WINTER in Dimwood Forest. Temperatures were low, snows deep, nights long, and the winds sharp. Most forest animals remained tucked away in their underground homes, burrows, and caves, sleeping or eating the food they had stored the summer before. It was that way, too, with Poppy and Rye, who kept close and warm deep down among the roots of their old snag, a tall, broken tree stump.

Poppy, an elderly deer mouse, had curled herself up into a plump ball of tan fur, her tail wrapped about so that it touched the tip of her pink nose. She was chatting with her husband, Rye, about some of the events of the past year: their good life together; guiding and watching their children grow and begin families of their own; her visit to her old home, Gray House; renewing acquaintances with

relatives; and happy times with Ereth the porcupine.

As she talked, Rye, a golden mouse, was lying on his back, eyes closed, paws beneath his head, tail occasionally twitching. He was listening to Poppy even as he was contemplating a new poem, something about the cold winter and the past summer.

"It's no good," Rye said quite suddenly while coming to his feet.

"What's no good?" asked Poppy, thinking he was referring to her talk about the family picnic last autumn.

"If I'm going to write anything decent about winter," Rye declared, "I need to get out there and experience it."

"It's awfully cold," Poppy reminded him, perfectly aware that such practical notions would make no difference to Rye, not when he was thinking about a poem. "I think there's a storm."

"Won't be a moment," said Rye, and he headed for the steps that led to ground level. When he reached the snag's open entryway, however, the storm's bitter cold struck with such force that it momentarily took his breath away. Not to be deterred, Rye pushed through the snow that had drifted in, and stepped outside.

It was difficult to see anything. The snow, bright and whirling, made the land indistinguishable from the sky. Even the forest trees appeared to be trembling shadows. As for sound, the only thing Rye could hear was the yowl of the wind.

"Wonderful . . . ," he murmured, even as he shivered and stepped forward, sinking deeply into a soft, powdery drift.

He brushed the flakes from his eyelashes, and they danced before his eyes like tiny, sparkling diamonds.

"Beautiful," he murmured.

Rye began to burrow forward with his front paws. As he tunneled into the snow, the sounds of the wind faded. The light turned a dull gray. The cold softened. It was as if he were in a cocoon made of winter.

Suddenly he halted. Embedded in the icy tunnel wall was a perfectly preserved green leaf.

"Oh my!" Rye whispered, gazing at the leaf with joy. "It's from last summer!"

Rye remained looking at the leaf for a long while. Only when his toes started to become numb did he turn and scurry back down into the snag.

"I think I've got a good poem," he announced as he returned to Poppy. "I'm going to call it 'Ice Leaf.'" He threw himself down on his back and closed his eyes.

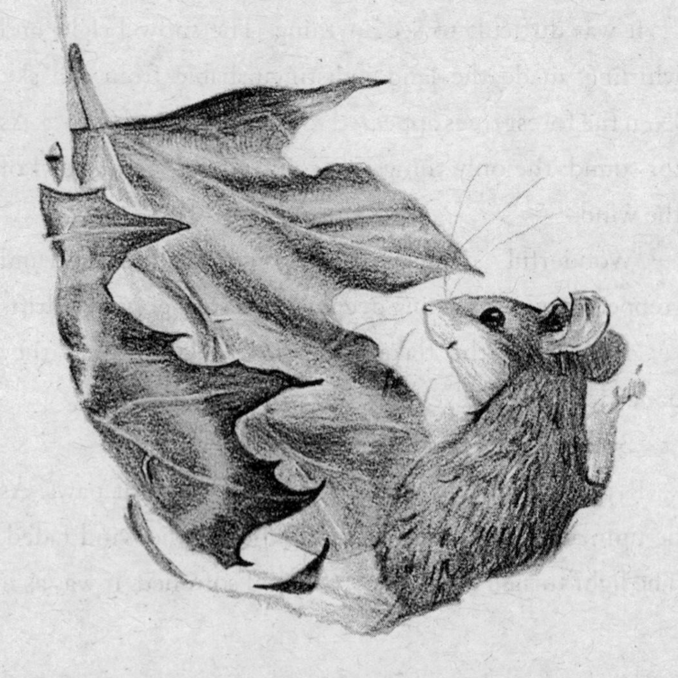

After a few moments he asked, "Do you have any more of your mix?"

"What mix?" said Poppy.

"That peppermint, elderberry, and honey mix. You know, for coughs."

Poppy's brow furrowed. "Why?"

"Slight tingle in the old throat," muttered Rye, as he concentrated on his poem.

That night a fierce new storm swept in. The wind roared. The temperature plummeted. The two mice snuggled together for warmth. From somewhere far-off they heard a fox baying and an owl hooting.

Next morning, when Rye woke, his throat was very sore. He was coughing, too, coughing badly.

CHAPTER 2

Junior Brings Ereth Some News

A WEEK LATER, early morning, a mouse called Junior, his fur encrusted with snow, managed to make his way into Ereth's smelly log. The old porcupine was sound asleep, snoring loudly.

After a moment's hesitation, Junior patted him on the nose. "Uncle Ereth!" he said. "Wake up, please!"

Ereth opened one eye. "Who . . . who's that?"

"It's me, Junior. Poppy's son."

"Growling gingersnaps . . . it's a bit early, isn't it?"

"Uncle Ereth, you're Poppy's best friend. I'm sure you'll want to know."

"Want to know what?" the porcupine grumbled.

"It's Rye—my father. Last night . . . he . . . died."

Ereth jerked up his head. "*What?*" he cried. "Rye? D-dead? But . . . but he's . . . so young!"

"Well, yes, he was."

"Then how—?"

"You know Rye," said Junior. "He went out into a storm looking for poetic inspiration. Stayed out too long. Developed a cough. The cough worsened and settled in his chest. A fever came on next. The fever became pneumonia. Mom nursed him tenderly, but . . . last night I'm afraid he . . . died in her paws. She wanted you to know."

"Sorry," mumbled Ereth.

"Thanks. Afraid I can't talk more," said Junior, retreating. "I need to get back to her."

"Right. Sure."

Alone, Ereth scratched his belly. He looked up. He looked down. He closed his eyes and then opened them. He shook his head as if something was irritating an ear or his brain. "What's the point of living," he muttered, "if all you do is get old and . . . die?"

Ereth recalled that Poppy's children had gone off with spouses and had families of their own. She would be alone. "She needs me," he announced with sudden urgency.

Quills rattling, the porcupine heaved himself up and walked unsteadily to the entrance of his log. Once there he gazed out upon the spotless white landscape. Large white flakes were drifting down with such gentleness that they blended into a soft blanket of thick silence.

Resolutely, if slowly, Ereth pushed his way through the high snowdrifts. By the time he reached Poppy's snag, his quills were laden with snow and ice, his eyes were blurred with tears, and his black nose stung from the cold.

Since the hole through which Poppy and Rye entered the snag was too small for Ereth to get through, he had to stop. "Poppy!" he bellowed. "It's me! Ereth! I want to tell you how badly I feel!"

After what seemed to be a long time, one of Poppy and Rye's daughters, Mariposa, appeared.

"Oh, hello, Uncle Ereth."

Disappointed it was not Poppy, Ereth mumbled, "Just wanted to say . . . I'm . . . I'm sorry. About Rye."

"Well . . . thank you. It is sad."

"Listen here; I forgot your name—"

"Mariposa."

"I need to speak to Poppy."

Mariposa was silent.

"You have some problem with that?" demanded Ereth.

"Uncle Ereth," Mariposa whispered, "why don't you come back a little later? Poppy is—"

"What?"

"She wants to be alone. Quiet. I'm sure you can understand."

"But . . ."

"Uncle Ereth, please."

Ereth began to say something but instead wheeled about and started back through the snow. Halfway home he paused. "Maybe I shouldn't have been so loud, so—" He did not finish the thought.

Back in his log, Ereth shook off the snow and retreated to the far end. "I suppose I should have been softer," he muttered as he hunkered down. "Or expressed more sympathy with . . . some . . . niceness. Dying . . . it's so . . . *stupid.*" He closed his eyes and sighed.

Five days passed before Ereth went back outside. He searched and scratched about the snowy forest until he found an old pinecone that had a few remaining seeds. Clutching it in his chattering teeth, he lumbered to Poppy's snag.

"Poppy!" he called. "Poppy!"

Though no answer came, Ereth waited until he could no longer bear the cold. Leaving the pinecone at the entryway to the snag, he stumbled home. Two days later, he returned. The pinecone was gone. But when he called for Poppy, there was still no reply.

Ereth waited a whole week before making his next visit. When he called for Poppy, still no one answered. This time Ereth did something he had never done before: he left a bit of his favorite food, salt, by her snag.

Two weeks later Ereth went back. The salt was exactly where he had left it. Ereth, who was quite capable of passing the whole of winter without speaking to another creature, was anxious.

"Poppy!" he bellowed. "I have to see you!"

Poppy appeared. Ereth stared at his friend. She was thin. Her whiskers drooped. Her eyes seemed dull. She kept rubbing her forepaws together as if they were cold.

"Yes, Ereth," she said, speaking softly. "Can I help you?"

"I just wanted . . . to . . . say . . . I'm really sorry. About Rye."

"Yes. Thank you. It's . . . hard."

"I left . . . some things."

"The pinecone. That was very kind. As for the salt . . . I'm afraid I don't really care for salt. Why don't you take it back? I know how much you love it." Poppy's voice was so low, Ereth could barely hear her words.

"I just . . . thought," Ereth stammered, "we might do . . . something to—"

"Ereth," said Poppy, "I need to be alone for a while."

"How come?"

"I'd . . . like to spend some time reading Rye's poetry," she said. Eyes welling with tears, she hastily turned and disappeared from view.

Ereth stared at the salt. Though just to look at it made him salivate, he was not going to take it back. As far as he was concerned, it belonged to Poppy. But otherwise the porcupine had no choice. He felt compelled to respect Poppy's wishes.

"Dancing doorknobs," he muttered as he trudged back home to his log. "I'm supposed to be her best friend!

How can she not want to see me? It's as if she's gone away—permanently."

It was not the cold that made Ereth shiver: it was the thought.

CHAPTER 3

Changes

THOUGH THE DAYS grew longer, the weather remained bitterly cold and snowy for weeks. Then, like the sudden turn of an aspen leaf in a puff of wind, the weather changed. Skies cleared. The sun became bright. The temperature climbed. Within a few weeks, unseasonable warmth and slashing torrents of rain melted the winter's deepest snow. Streams crested. Mud oozed. Tree leaves dripped and dripped. Frogs sang with joy.

The rains finally ended, but the heat continued to rise. Spring hardly arrived before it fled. In its place came an early and *hot* summer, hotter than anyone could remember. Flowers wilted. Green shoots collapsed. Mushrooms shriveled.

Midsummer brought no improvement. Hot, then hotter; dry, and drier yet. The forest floor became hard.

Grasses turned brown. Tree leaves fell. Creeks turned into empty gullies. No doubt a drought had come to the forest.

And in all this time Ereth did not see Poppy.

CHAPTER 4

Spruce and Poppy

SPRUCE WAS THE SON of Ragweed Junior and Laurel. Not only had he been the last of his litter to be born that spring, he was small and skinny. His siblings called him the runt of the family though never when their parents were around.

Spruce generally enjoyed being with his brothers and sisters, but with food scarce because of the dry summer, he often found himself pushed aside or at the end of the line for good seeds. It may have happened less than he thought, but it was all too frequent for him. The result: though he was hardly more than three months old, he took to going off by himself and wandering about in search of something to eat.

One morning during the middle of summer, despite

the intense heat, Spruce set out alone. After some hours of searching, he found a dry pine seed. He was just about to eat it when he saw his grandmother Poppy coming along the path.

Spruce's parents had told their children not to bother Grandma Poppy because she was so sad about Rye's death and wanted to be left alone. It had happened before Spruce was born, so although he had heard of Poppy's many adventures, he hardly knew her. Mostly, he thought of her as very old, and Spruce was uncertain how he felt about old mice.

"Good morning, Grandma," he whispered as he stepped aside to let Poppy pass while eyeing her with curiosity.

Poppy went silently by only to halt a few steps beyond, turn, and look back at the young mouse.

"Oh my," she said. "I have so many grandchildren. I can hardly count them and don't know them all by name. But I believe you are . . . Spruce. One of Junior and Laurel's sons. Am I right?"

"Yes, thank you," said Spruce, amazed that Grandma Poppy knew him at all.

Poppy gazed intently at the young mouse. "You resemble your father," she announced.

"I do?" asked Spruce, who had never thought he looked

like anyone except himself.

"And your father," continued Poppy, "looked like *his* father. That means you are rather like your grandfather Rye. But the more I consider it, the one I think you most look like is your great-uncle Ragweed."

"Is that bad?" asked Spruce.

"Actually," said Poppy with an all but silent sigh, "I think it's . . . nice. Now tell me, Spruce, what are you doing out here alone on such a hot day?"

Spruce thought for a moment and then said, "I'm hunting foxes."

"Are you really?" Poppy cried.

"I saw a huge one go by a little while ago," said Spruce. "But, guess what? I chased him away."

"What a good story! What else have you been doing?"

"Looking for seeds."

"Find any?"

Spruce held up the seed he had found. "Would you like a bite?"

Poppy actually smiled, something she had not done for a long while. Spruce's offer somehow made her feel lighter.

"Spruce," she said, "what would you say to my helping you look for more seeds?"

Spruce was surprised. As far as he knew, Poppy had

never spent any time with his brothers or sisters. "Do you really want to?" he asked.

Poppy nodded. "And if we see another fox," she added solemnly, "I'll help you chase him away. I think that would be really fun."

"I'd like that," said Spruce, delighted that Poppy enjoyed his joke.

All that afternoon Poppy and Spruce searched about the forest. They talked very little, and mostly about Spruce, but they did manage to avoid all foxes even as they collected some seeds. Then Poppy led Spruce to a rock under which they could sit in the cool shade.

"Spruce," said Poppy as they ate, "what do you like to do most of all?"

"I don't know . . . ," the young mouse mused. "Probably doing something nobody else does. Just me. All alone."

Poppy looked around at him. To Spruce she seemed very serious. "Is that bad?" he asked.

"Oh no!" cried Poppy. "You know, your great-uncle Ragweed—the one you look like—he used to say, 'A mouse has to do what a mouse has to do.'"

"'A mouse has to do what a mouse has to do,'" Spruce repeated. "I like that." And he gazed at Poppy and struggled to understand what it was like to be so old. Next moment he blurted out, "Then what is it *you* have to do?"

"Me?" said Poppy, taken aback by the question. "What do you mean?"

"It's what you said, about a mouse doing. . . . Only I guess you're . . . too old to do anything."

"Oh dear! Do I look that old?"

"Your whiskers droop."

"I suppose they do," said Poppy, not sure if she should laugh or cry. Instead, she sighed, half longingly, half resigned. "Well, I have to admit I'm not sure what I'll do."

"That's okay," said Spruce. "You're so old you don't *have* to do anything. Only I still think you should do *something*."

"Why?"

Spruce thought a moment. "Because I like you."

"Well, thank you!"

Later, as they parted, Spruce said, "Grandma Poppy . . . Mom and Dad told us not to bother you."

"Did they give a reason?"

"Because you were so sad."

"Ah," said Poppy. "I suppose I am."

"But, can I still . . . visit you?"

Poppy smiled. "Anytime you want. My snag is nice and cool—and empty."

"Okay," said Spruce, and off he went.

As Poppy watched him go she thought, *Now there's a charming young mouse. And he really does look like Ragweed.*

It made her think of Ragweed's words again—the words she had quoted to the young mouse: "*A mouse has to do what a mouse has to do.*" That, in turn, made her ponder the question Spruce had asked: "*Then what is it* you *have to do?*"

All the way back to the snag the question kept rolling about Poppy's head. Then, as she stepped into her home, she considered what Spruce had also said: "*You're so old you don't* have *to do anything.*"

It's true, thought Poppy. *These days all I'm doing is feeling hot, heavy, and tired.*

She set about straightening up the snag, but stopped and sat down and thought about Spruce instead. She had not been very much older than the young mouse when she met Ragweed. Closing her eyes, Poppy recalled the first time she saw Ragweed coming through the forest. Not only was his fur golden in color—something she had never seen before—he was singing and—oh, yes!—wearing a purple-beaded earring!

Poppy giggled. That earring . . . Ragweed had been her first love. Except, as she thought about it, it was not so much Ragweed she'd loved as his great love of life, his *energy*.

Poppy dug deeper into her memories. What *was* it like in those days when she began to spend time with Ragweed?

Certainly, her life had begun to change. She had started asking questions. She had grown a little bolder. Then Ragweed died tragically. But his death led to her meeting Ereth and her great duel with Mr. Ocax, the owl. That, in turn, brought her to Rye, with whom she fell in love.

Rye had cared so much about life, and about Poppy, too, as well as about poetry and their family—all in the sweetest of ways. No, nothing flamboyant about Rye—just a steady, kind, and loving mouse. Oh, how she missed him!

How different my life used to be, thought Poppy. *So many changes! Now I am utterly predictable!* Nothing *varies!* She shrugged. *It certainly would be nice if days were cooler and something different happened.*

Poppy went back to thinking about Ragweed's earring. *It's almost,* she thought, *as if that tiny twist of metal with its small purple bead was the spark that altered my life!*

What ever did become of that earring? Poppy mused. Next moment she remembered: she had hung it on a hazelnut tree atop Bannock Hill so she would always remember Ragweed.

She gasped. *But life became so busy I did forget about that earring!*

All at once, Poppy felt an overwhelming desire to see if the earring was where she had put it. Never mind the heat. Never mind the lateness of the day. She must see if it was still there. In her mind, she again heard Spruce say, *"You're so old you don't* have *to do anything."*

"No!" Poppy cried right out loud. "I need to see if that earring is still there!"

The next moment she burst out of her snag and began to scurry along the path that would lead her through the forest, across Glitter Creek, and up to Bannock Hill.

As Poppy scampered along, she could not help but notice how grim the forest looked—so brittle and dusty that nothing moved without crinkling. While there was still a little greenery, much of the forest seemed rusty and stiff.

Poppy came to a halt. "Stop thinking droopy thoughts!" she scolded herself. "Be cheerful!"

She began to run and soon reached the banks of Glitter Creek. Before her lay the old bridge, and beyond, Bannock Hill. Too excited to even look at the creek, she dashed over to the other side.

What a comfort it will be if Ragweed's earring is still there, Poppy kept thinking as she raced toward the summit of the hill. "Oh, please, please," she said aloud, "*please* be there! I don't want everything to have changed!"

CHAPTER 5

Ereth Has Some Thoughts

DEEP INSIDE HIS HOLLOW LOG, Ereth chewed loudly on an old twig. He kept wishing the wood had even a tiny bit of green underbark for him to enjoy. In fact, the twig was no tastier than old chalk, so dry it hurt his teeth, so dry he could not even spit.

"Octopus ink ice cream," he muttered. "It needs salt, too."

Thoughts of salt made Ereth groan. As far as he was concerned, salt was the best-tasting food in the world. It had been such a long time since Ereth had eaten good salt, or any salt for that matter. He had left his last bit with Poppy.

Normally, his log home was damp and moldy, too, thick with the heavy reek of rot and poop. Ereth liked it that way. But the summer's unrelenting heat had turned

Ereth's log into an oven, an oven filled with sand. The enticing smells he so loved had all been baked out.

And now, there was no rain.

"What good is the sky if no rain falls from it?" Ereth complained, swishing his tail so hard his quills rattled. He wished someone would dare to contradict him. Since he was alone, no one did.

"It's *stupid* that it doesn't rain," Ereth rambled on, licking his parched black lips. "It's not as if the sky has anything better to do! The forest needs rain. Animals need rain. Spider snot soup!" he bleated. "*I* need rain!"

Exasperated, he threw down the twig he had been chewing. "I can't eat junk!" he cried. "Creamed caterpillar cheese on chocolate-coated cats! Even my quills are sweating! I need fresh air!"

Ereth waddled clumsily to the entrance of his log and stuck out his blunt, grizzled nose. He sniffed. The late afternoon air was as thick as greasy sheep's wool. Everywhere he looked he saw dry leaves, dry grass, dry *everything*. "It's all one big sawdust and sandpaper sandwich," he panted.

Ereth tried not to look toward Poppy's snag. Unable to resist, he peeked across. How he wished that Poppy would emerge and announce she was done with her sadness!

Next moment he was distracted from his longing by the sight of a bat darting about above him. "Bottled bat boogers," he muttered as he eyed the bat with distaste. "I hate bats. Everybody does."

He turned back to Poppy's snag with a new thought. "Maybe . . . Poppy thinks of me the way I . . . think of bats. With *disgust*! Maybe she doesn't want to see me, not because of Rye's death but because . . . because she doesn't like me anymore!"

The thought brought pain to his heart. "She probably finds me dull, or stupid, or rude. Too loud. Too unrefined. Too . . . me!

"Things have to change. No! Maybe *I* . . . need to change. First, I'll stop waiting for Poppy to come around. I'll get out and about. Make some . . . new friends. Mingle with . . . other animals. Be social. Go to parties. Dance. Make small talk. Have fun! Maybe I should even stop swearing! Maybe I should start"—the word almost made him gag—*"smiling!"*

"Yes," cried the porcupine with growing excitement. "Phooey on Poppy," he cried. "Fried figs on frog flop! No! No more swearing! Swearing is *stupid*! Smiles are sweet! Poppy can stew in her own sadness for all I care. I need new friends!"

As Ereth spoke, a hot wind blew dust into his mouth and snout. "No!" Ereth bleated to nobody in particular. "I need coolness. Wetness! A fresh bath will give my new personality the right start. I'll wash away my old self! But where can I take a bath? *Glitter Creek!* Yes!" And with a swish of his tail, Ereth headed for the path that led to the creek and began to run.

As Ereth rushed through the forest, his only thought was of the creek, which ran along the eastern edge of Dimwood

Forest. He could almost see the fresh, cool water frothing and tumbling over rocks and fallen branches, gurgling with the joy of racing against itself, as if the creek had turned itself into a smile. Yes, a smile! *Just like I'll be doing. And oh! A cool, wet bath would be so silky sweet! Something worth smiling about!*

The pleasures of becoming wet, of a bath, of soaking in the clear creek waters made Ereth fairly gallop along, thinking, *Pickled pink potatoes! No! Mustn't swear anymore. Never again! Still, I'll take a swim. Don't do it often, but I can and . . . I . . . I will! The perfect time!*

He paid little attention to the heat, the wilted grass, or the drooping forest trees.

Maybe, thought Ereth, *I should live closer to the creek. Take a bath every day. Not to be clean. Phooey on clean! But oh, oh! To be cool!*

At last Ereth saw the open space that meant he was approaching the creek. Sweat trickled down over his eyes, stinging them, obscuring his vision. Not that Ereth cared. All he could think about, all he wanted, all he needed was to plunge into the creek's crisp, cool waters.

He dashed forward.

When Ereth finally reached the creek bank, he, without bothering to look, leaped—only to land with a sickening *splat!* right in a bed of thick, deep, engulfing mud.

Ereth floundered in the mire, spitting out the sandy grit that seeped into his mouth. He began to churn his rear legs to get out. The churning only made him slip deeper into the goo.

"Barbecued buzzard barf!" Ereth screeched. "Help!" he bellowed. "Somebody! Anybody! Poppy! Save me! I'm drowning!"

CHAPTER 6

Ragweed's Earring

Poppy sat atop Bannock Hill gazing up at the twilight blue sky. Not a single cloud that might bring a drop of cooling rain was in sight. To the west, the setting sun was so brutally hot, it was as if it *wanted* to scorch the earth, as if it *wanted* to suck up every last measure of moisture from the parched forest, as if it *wanted* to toast the world into a crusty crisp. It made Poppy's eyes ache.

She shifted her gaze and scrutinized the limp, dry leaves of the nearby hazelnut tree. In the slanting rays of the setting sun, something on a high branch glittered like a small star. Her heart gave a thump of recognition.

It is there! Ragweed's earring! Just where I put it so long ago! Oh my, and thank goodness. Some things do not *change! I really should bring Spruce here and show it to him. He needs to know about his great-uncle and about how I first came to Dimwood Forest.*

How did I get here? She tried to recall.

Memories flooded back: how she had risked the dangerous crossing over Glitter Creek and then entered Dimwood Forest for the first time. *Yes,* Poppy decided—*crossing the creek, that's when my old life ended and my real life truly began.*

A thought struck her: *Perhaps if I returned to Glitter Creek I could start a new life once again.*

Poppy smiled sadly, perfectly aware that she was being sentimental, foolishly so. *It's too late to change who I am, an ordinary-looking deer mouse with tan fur on my back, a plump white belly, and thinning, drooping gray whiskers. I just hope my black eyes are still sharp. Silly mouse!* she chided herself. *You're too old to start anything new!*

Suddenly she felt as if the whole world were reaching down and pressing a heavy paw atop her head. The notion brought tears to her eyes. "I don't want to be sad anymore," she said aloud. "I want to be cheerful."

Poppy wiped her tears away with a paw. At least Glitter Creek with its clear, bright waters might lighten her mood. Not allowing herself second thoughts, she whispered, "I'll go right now!" and hurried down Bannock Hill.

Poppy felt a flutter of excitement, as if she were about to see an old friend after a long time. But even as she hurried on, she heard a faint cry. "Help! Somebody! Anybody! Poppy! Save me! I'm drowning!" It was coming from straight ahead. From Glitter Creek! And she was being called!

Poppy raced along, her tail stretched out straight behind her. Darting across Tar Road, she quickly reached the banks of the creek.

Or what had been the creek. She saw now that the awful heat had dried up most of the water. All that remained were a few shallow puddles of stagnant brown water. Grasses had wilted. Not a single water lily was in sight. No water bugs, either. A few dead fish—white bellies turned up—dotted the mud. The air stank of decay and rot. Most of all, there was a vast amount of thick, gooey mud. And half buried in the mud was Ereth.

Mud speckled his face, ears, eyes, and quills. He kept spitting mud, too. And as Ereth thrashed frantically about, he kept sinking deeper.

"Help!" he cried. "Help!"

He looked so much like a muddy pincushion that Poppy burst out laughing—not just one short snort of laughter but laughter that was impossible to stop.

Hearing Poppy's merriment, Ereth stopped struggling

and blinked away the mud from his eyes.

"Poppy!" he screamed. "You stinky slurp of scab stew! Don't just stand there! Save me!"

"But . . . what are you doing?" she replied, still laughing.

"What do you think I'm doing? I'm *drowning*!" Even as Ereth cried out, he sank a little deeper.

Poppy, now fully realizing the porcupine's predicament, called, "Ereth! Don't struggle so! It's making you sink faster!"

"But if I do nothing, I'll sink anyway!" sputtered the increasingly panicked Ereth.

"I'll think of something," Poppy assured him, and she looked about to see what she could use to help.

Spying a dead branch on the creek bank, she ran to it and tried to push it toward Ereth. The branch, however, proved too heavy for the small mouse to budge.

Searching with greater urgency, Poppy noticed a tree growing out of the bank, its branches hanging over the creek bed. If she could move one of those branches low enough for Ereth to grab, he should be able to haul himself to safety.

"Hold on!" she cried.

"To what?" screeched the porcupine. "There's nothing to hold but mud!"

"I'm getting something," cried Poppy, and she scampered over to the tree, climbed its trunk, and ran swiftly out along one of its long, slender branches. When Poppy reached its end, the branch did bow down toward Ereth, but not nearly close enough for him to grab.

"Are you going to help me?" Ereth screamed.

"I'm trying!" called Poppy. "But I'm too light!"

"Then get fatter, you dangle of duck drool! Or I'll disappear!"

Poppy looked around again. Farther back on the branch where she stood, an abandoned bird's nest was wedged into a fork.

She glanced at the ground. Small rocks and pebbles were scattered along the exposed creek bank. "Don't worry!" she called. "I think I know how to save you!"

CHAPTER 7

A Surprise

POPPY TORE DOWN TO THE GROUND, snatched up a pebble in her mouth, dashed back up, ran out along the branch, and spat the small stone into the nest. Then she ran down to the ground again and grabbed another.

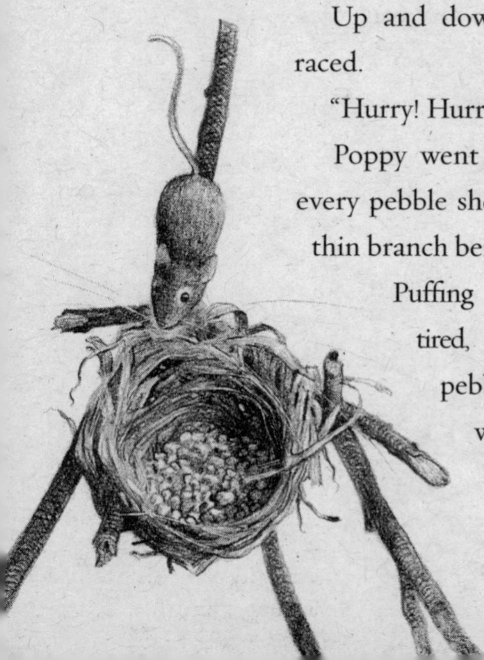

Up and down and back and forth she raced.

"Hurry! Hurry!" Ereth kept calling.

Poppy went as fast as she could. With every pebble she dropped into the nest, the thin branch bent a little lower.

Puffing with exertion, and growing tired, Poppy dropped yet another pebble into the nest. The branch was now deeply bowed but still not quite low enough for Ereth to grasp. To make matters worse, the porcupine had sunk even deeper into the mud.

Poppy saw just one more possibility. She raced to the end of the branch, grabbed hold of its tip with two paws, and let herself dangle. With the added weight, the branch dipped lower, just over Ereth's head.

As she hung there, Poppy shouted, "Ereth! You must get one of your paws free of the mud! Reach up! Try to take hold of the branch! Just don't grab me!"

While Ereth made a great effort to do as he was told, Poppy began to pump her legs up and down, building momentum so as to bring the branch still lower.

Finally yanking his right paw free, Ereth stretched up. The bobbing branch and his claws remained inches apart; he could not grab it.

"Keep trying!" yelled Poppy as she pumped her legs even more vigorously so that the branch bobbed lower and lower. Every time the branch dipped, Ereth snatched wildly at it only to miss—although once or twice his claws scraped the wood just above Poppy's paws.

As Poppy worked harder, Ereth stretched as far as he could with his paw and . . . "Got it!" he cried at last.

"Now!" Poppy shouted. "Grab hold with *two* paws.

Then haul yourself up!"

Using the branch for leverage, Ereth pulled another paw free from the mud and seized the branch firmly with two paws.

Though the clumps of wet mud sticking to his prickly back made him extremely heavy, Ereth began to heave himself out of the creek.

"Pull harder!" yelled Poppy.

Ereth continued to pull up on the branch until he was out of the mud.

"Now," Poppy urged, her own rear legs just grazing above the mud, "move toward dry land."

Clinging to the branch, Ereth edged toward the creek bank.

"You're almost there!" Poppy shouted.

The moment Ereth saw that he was over firm ground he let go of the branch.

But as Ereth fell, the branch whipped up like the released arm of a catapult. The sudden movement caught Poppy completely by surprise, flinging her with such enormous force that she went shooting straight up in the air.

"Oh my goodness!" Poppy gasped as the wind rippled through her fur and bent back her whiskers. "I'm flying!" Sure enough, she was soaring up in the air, dizzyingly high.

She darted a look below. From the banks of Glitter Creek, Ereth was staring up at her, openmouthed in astonishment. Even in the moment she looked at him, he became smaller.

Poppy glanced toward the west. The twilight sky offered a glowing sunset—all red, purple, and orange.

"Oh my!" she cried. "So this is what the sky is like. It's really quite lovely. And flying is very cooling. No wonder birds like it."

Poppy looked down again. The individual treetops were melding together to become a vast expanse. "Goodness! It's the entire forest!" she exclaimed. "How different everything looks from a distance!"

Then she felt herself slowing. That brought a frightful realization: *If I stop rising, I'll start falling. And since I've gone up such a long way, when I hit the ground it will most likely be the death of me.*

For a fraction of a second, Poppy hung suspended in

the air. Then she began to drop—plummeting faster and faster. Though her heart pounded, and she closed her eyes, her thoughts were very clear: *Who would have ever guessed that I'd end my life by falling out of the sky?*

CHAPTER 8

Luci in the Sky

POPPY WAS STILL FALLING when she suddenly felt her skin pricked and then grabbed. Not only did she stop dropping, she was actually rising in short, jerky movements.

Bewildered, she opened her eyes. She was being *held* higher than she had been before. The forest below was moving by very quickly. *I'm not going to die by falling,* she decided. *I'm going to be eaten by some bird.*

She twisted her head around and looked up. To her complete surprise, the creature carrying her was *not* a bird. At first glance it appeared to be a *mouse*! Not much bigger than she, it had brown fur and bright black eyes. But the creature's nose was large for its pushed-in face, had flaring nostrils, and was not sharp like a mouse's. Its ears were very large and pointy.

Most astonishing of all were the great leathery wings

extending from the creature's body, wings that whipped the air with such rapidity they were hard to see.

A bat had grabbed her.

Poppy quickly recalled the things she had heard about bats—that they were strange, perhaps even magical creatures given to violent and erratic mischief; that they guided themselves through the air in a mystifying fashion; that bats, for no good reason at all, constantly attacked other creatures—even ate them!—and that they entangled themselves in animals' fur, biting, scratching, and spreading all kinds of ghastly diseases. In short, bats were to be absolutely avoided.

What to do? Clearly, she could not get away, not unless she wanted to fall. Perhaps speaking to the frightful thing would help.

Poppy took a deep breath and called up, "Hello, there! Can you hear me?"

"Oh hi!" the bat squeaked. "Were you talking to me?"

"I was," said Poppy. "Are you a bat?"

"Oh sure."

"What's your name?"

"My full name is Myotis Lucifugus. But my friends call me Luci."

"*Luci?*"

"I think it's nicer than Fugus," the bat went on. "Or My.

And Otis is a boy's name and I'm a girl. Oh, what's your name?"

"Poppy."

"Boy or girl?"

"Well . . . girl."

"*Miss* Poppy! I like that."

"I suppose I should thank you for catching me," said Poppy. "Otherwise I'd have fallen. Probably been killed."

"That would have been awful," agreed Luci.

Poppy hesitated for a moment and then said, "Luci, why did you grab me?"

"What a question," said Luci, her voice full of surprise. "What do you think? Because I'm going to eat you."

"*Eat me?*" cried Poppy, her worst fears confirmed. "Why would you want to do that?"

"I think everyone eats something," said Luci, only to add, "Don't they?"

"I suppose," admitted Poppy, "but I don't think you'd get much pleasure in eating an old mouse."

"*Mouse!*" cried Luci. "No way! Are you a *mouse? Really?*"

"From the tip of my nose to the tip of my tail!" Poppy hastened to say.

"Miss Poppy," squeaked the bat. "I am *so* embarrassed! This is my first solo flight and I thought you were a . . . a moth."

"How could you possibly mistake me for a moth!" Poppy sputtered.

"Well, there you were, right up in the air over the forest," said Luci. "That's where moths are, right? They are really tasty." The bat giggled. "See, I've never met a mouse before! But now I know that mice fly, too. I'd be happy to let you go." Luci started to loosen her grip.

"No, don't!" cried Poppy. "I can't fly!"

"Can't you?" said the bat. "Then . . . then how did you get up in the air?"

"It's . . . it's too hard to explain," said Poppy, looking down at the darkening earth. "Do you think you could just put me on the ground, gently?"

"Sorry," said Luci. "I can't. I'm late."

"Late for what?"

"Mom told me to take my first flight, grab a snack if I could, and then get back home. I know. Hard to believe that at my age I actually have a curfew—but I do."

"How old are you?" Poppy asked.

"Three weeks."

"And did you say this was your first flight?"

"Really exciting, isn't it?" said the bat as she made a sudden sharp turn, abrupt enough to startle Poppy.

Poppy, resigned to being carried along, caught her breath and looked down and about. The last rays of the setting sun were cutting across Dimwood's treetops so that the whole forest seemed edged with gold. The sky had been transformed into a panoramic, multihued rainbow of blue, orange, and pink. *How huge the sky is!* thought Poppy. *How beautiful. This is certainly a lovely way to see the world!*

As always, seeing something lovely made Poppy think of Rye, who would have written a poem about such an extraordinary sight. But these pleasant thoughts were cut short when Luci abruptly plunged to a lower altitude. They were now just skimming over the treetops.

"Oh my!" exclaimed Poppy, almost breathless.

"Am I flying poorly?" Luci asked.

"Just fine," Poppy managed. She tried to determine where she was, telling herself she would need to return home on her own. Luci, however, was going so fast it was hard to pick out landmarks. Besides, the sun was all but down. The only light was coming from the far west.

Luci dipped deeper among the tall, dark trees, darting around them with such sharp turns and shifts, Poppy became giddy. "Do you live in a tree?" she asked.

"Oh no, we live in a cave."

Even as she spoke, the young bat broke away from the trees. Flying swiftly if somewhat erratically, Luci was now heading right toward a high cliff. As far as Poppy could see, it was a wall of solid stone.

"Luci!" cried Poppy. "There's a rock cliff straight ahead! Shouldn't you turn?"

"I don't think so," said Luci, continuing to fly straight toward the face of the rock.

Poppy had no doubt the young bat was about to crash. She closed her eyes and said, "Good-bye, world!"

CHAPTER 9

What Ereth Thought He Saw

"I'M SAFE!" Ereth shouted when he plumped down from the branch and landed on the creek bank. With a quick shake of his head, body, and tail, he flung off the mud that coated him. Only then did he look around for Poppy. He was actually going to thank her.

Poppy, however, was nowhere to be seen.

Puzzled, Ereth peered up at the branch that Poppy had managed to pull down. That was when he saw his friend streaking straight up into the twilight sky.

"*Poppy?*" he gasped, watching with disbelief as the mouse soared upward. "Is that . . . *you?*"

Ereth stared into the sky until the mouse appeared to stop rising and then began to fall.

The porcupine held his breath.

The very next moment *something*—Ereth wasn't sure

what it was or even if it *was* something—appeared out of the sky, snatched Poppy away, and then—*vanished.*

Astonished, Ereth could not move. Instead, he continued to study the darkening sky where Poppy had been. *Was that truly Poppy? If it was Poppy, how did she get up there? And if she did get up there, what happened to her?*

Baffled, Ereth continued to stare at the sky, not sure he could—or should—believe what he had seen. *Did I imagine everything?* Ereth asked himself. *Was I missing Poppy so much I just dreamed she saved me?* No! He had seen Poppy rising into the sky, only to disappear!

No! That was impossible. But then, where was she?

Utterly mystified, the porcupine searched about the creek bank. He studied the mud. He scrutinized the sky again. Not a single sign of Poppy did he find.

I must, he decided, *have imagined it all. A mouse in the sky . . . flying . . . disappearing . . . that's just not . . . possible. . . . Unless I'm crazy.*

Determined to convince himself that he had only imagined what had happened, Ereth galloped home, taking pains to follow the exact route he had used when coming to Glitter Creek.

It was dark and Ereth was quite worn-out when he reached the foot of Poppy's snag.

"Poppy!" he cried. "Come out! It's me, Ereth!"

There was no reply.

"Poppy!" he shouted with a mix of agony and rage. "Answer me!"

Still no answer.

"Poppy!" Ereth pleaded. "*Please*! All I ask is that you tell me you're here! That you're safe! Then I promise, I'll go away. Forever!"

He waited, all the while watching the snag intently. "Maybe she's just playing a trick on me," he muttered, hardly knowing whether to be frightened or furious but desperately wanting *some* explanation.

"Yes, that's it. She's playing a practical joke on me. As if it's funny to disappear like that. Leaving no trace. No note. Or words. No respect. No caring. No friendship. No love. No nothing! Well, I'll do the same. I'll ignore her. Forget her. Pluck her out of my memory. Out of my heart. Act as if she never existed. As if we never did anything together. As if I never cared for her. *Ever!*"

Sighing deeply, Ereth remained silent for a moment, only to lift his head and wail, "Poppy, *please* tell me what happened to you!

"But I do know what happened!" Ereth reminded himself. "She saved me and then went up in the air and . . . disappeared.

"But—how could that be?"

A new explanation formed in his mind. Perhaps Poppy had fallen into the creek and had sunk the way he did. In the twilight gloom he just hadn't noticed.

Ereth's heart gave a lurch. *I must still try to save her.*

He raced back to Glitter Creek. As he scurried along, his mind was a muddle of self-reproach: *I should have checked more. I should have searched harder. What a dunce I am! What an idiot! How cruel and unthinking! There I was, only thinking about myself. How selfish! How vain! How stupid! How like me!*

Panting and exhausted, Ereth reached the bank of the creek. Pale yellow moonlight filled the heavy, warm air and lay upon the empty creek bed like a golden carpet softening the rough edges of the drought-parched landscape. Crickets endlessly, mindlessly rubbed their legs together. Mosquitoes droned.

"Poppy!" Ereth cried into the darkness. "Are you here?

Are you drowning? Please, please, *please* tell me you are drowning—so I can save you!"

The last words were spoken in the feeblest of voices, a voice tinged with complete despair.

Bleary-eyed and quite frightened, Ereth attempted yet again to make sense of what had happened. He closed his eyes. It was too extraordinary. Too awful. Too dreadful. Even so, there were a couple of things about which he was now quite convinced: he had seen Poppy fly into the sky, and then she had disappeared.

Poppy, in order to save her best friend—*him*—had sacrificed herself.

The painful fact made him groan. But since he was now convinced of what had happened, Ereth made himself say aloud the awful words he was thinking: "While saving me, Poppy . . . *died*!"

As he spoke, he began to fully understand what he had witnessed. *Could it have been? Might it have been possible? There's no other explanation! What I saw rising into the sky must have been . . . was . . . Poppy's . . .* ghost*!*

CHAPTER 10

In the Dark

I'M STILL ALIVE! thought Poppy, even though she opened her eyes to complete blackness. Luci had not crashed into the stone cliff and they were still flying, but in a deeper darkness than Poppy had ever experienced. What's more, it was exceedingly cold.

"Hello! Luci!" she called. "Where are we?"

"Home," squeaked Luci.

"Where's home?" asked Poppy.

"Our cave."

"Is it big?"

"I guess," said Luci.

"Where are we going now?"

"Actually, Miss Poppy, I'm going to set you down," said the bat. "I don't mean to be disrespectful, but you're heavy."

"That sounds wonderful," said Poppy, wanting nothing

more than to feel solid earth under her paws. Her back was getting a little sore, too.

She sensed they were descending. Then her toes touched the ground.

"Are you all right?" the bat asked as she released Poppy.

"I think so," Poppy answered, a little breathless as she tried to stand on wobbly legs. Since she could not see anything, she felt about where she had landed. The surface was hard, with a cold, slippery dampness.

"Be back soon!" cried Luci. "Don't go anywhere!"

"But . . . !"

Poppy heard a flutter of wings, followed by a *whoosh* of wind—then silence. Presumably, the young bat was gone—though Poppy had not actually seen her go.

Trembling slightly with the chill, Poppy smoothed out her whiskers, flicked her ears, shook out her tail, and took a deep breath. *What a strange experience!* she thought as her heart resumed its normal rhythm. *First flying. Then to come to a place I can't see, surrounded by I don't know what, and not knowing what's going to happen next. I'd hide, but it's hard to hide since I can't see where I am to begin with.*

"Oh well," she said, finding comfort in talking aloud. "I am alive. I helped Ereth get out of that mud. I've experienced being in the sky. That bat did not eat me. I've gotten away from the terrible heat. Nothing bad in any of that.

As for Luci, what a pleasant name for such a creature. And actually, she's nice too. For a bat."

Poppy considered the question of other bats. *Perhaps not all bats are so friendly. What if Luci went to get them? No, I don't think I should relax too much.*

"Hello!" came a squeak close to her ears. "I'm back!"

Startled, Poppy gazed in the direction of the voice. "Who . . . who's there?" she asked.

"It's me, Miss Poppy. Luci."

"Oh," said Poppy. "I . . . I was wondering where you went. Are you . . . alone?"

"I fetched Mom," said Luci. "I really wanted her to meet you. She's right here."

"Hello," Poppy said, thinking how odd it was to greet someone she could not see. "My name is Poppy. I'm a deer mouse," she added in haste, wanting to make clear that she was *not* a moth. "I'm very pleased to meet you."

"How do you do, Miss Poppy?" returned a voice, high-pitched like Luci's. "My name is Miranda. Luci's mother. I hope you'll forgive her." The bat giggled. "She told me she thought you were a moth. We bats do of course eat insects: mosquitoes, moths, dragonflies, and the odd beetle, that sort of thing. Perhaps an occasional nip of nectar. But no mice," she said, giggling. "Oh my, gracious no."

"That's what Luci explained," said Poppy, wanting to

be as friendly as possible. "And, Miranda—may I call you that?—I do know the young make mistakes. I've had a few children myself."

"How many?" asked Miranda.

"Eleven."

"*Eleven?*" cried the bat, laughing. "Luci! Did you hear? Eleven children! Oh my! One a year is good enough for me, thank you. So far, just five. But eleven! The most astonishing thing I've ever heard." She laughed again.

Poppy, wondering what was so funny, only said, "Do you think it might be possible for me to get out of this cave?"

"You'd have to fly."

Poppy recognized Luci's voice.

"I'm sure Luci can take you back," Miranda said. "However, I think our little Luci is all tuckered out for today. You know, a first flight is always an exhausting adventure." She laughed. "Imagine Luci thinking you a moth! Anyway, tomorrow evening would be best. Now then, Miss Poppy, as for sleep, you're welcome to join us."

"How many of you are there?" asked Poppy.

"Oh, I couldn't even begin to count," said Miranda.

"If you join us, you'll see. It's very cozy," said Luci. "But you'll have to hang yourself."

"Hang myself?" said Poppy.

"Hold yourself on the wall."

"Thank you," said Poppy in haste. "I better stay here."

"Okay, then," said Miranda. "We'll see you tomorrow."

Next moment, Poppy heard a flutter of wings. She stared into the darkness. "Is . . . anybody here?"

"Just me," said Luci. "Miss Poppy, I just wanted to say again how dumb I was for thinking you were a moth. Can I help you with anything now?" she asked.

"Is there something to eat?" said Poppy.

"What do mice eat?"

"Seeds."

"Oh dear," said Luci. "I don't think we have any. Sorry! See you later. Bye!"

Poppy heard her flap into the air.

"What about some water?" Poppy called out. "I think I heard water trickling nearby!"

"Right over there!" came a distant call.

"Right over *where*?" No answer came. "Luci?" called Poppy. "Luci!"

But the young bat had apparently gone.

For a few moments, Poppy peered into the darkness. "Nothing to see," she whispered, though she did feel an occasional slight drift of cold air. "Nothing to eat." She listened hard, too, but aside from a tiny splash of water coming from somewhere, she felt surrounded by a great hollowness.

"No one to talk to, either." She sighed. "I'm not sure if I

should be frightened or not."

Since there was nothing to do but await Luci's return, Poppy curled up in a ball on the cold ground, tucked her nose into her belly, and wrapped her tail around herself. As she closed her eyes, she recalled how earlier that same day she'd wished that she were cool and that her life would change.

She sighed and, though feeling increasingly drowsy, said, "I certainly got my wish."

CHAPTER II

Above Dimwood Forest

High over Dimwood Forest, in the swirling mists of the night's deep darkness—very much higher than Poppy had flown—the day's thick humidity caused clouds, clogged with drought dust, to gather. The dust particles turned, tossed, and tumbled, rubbing one against another, and by so doing, charged the clouds with electricity. The electricity grew until it needed to release.

Atop Bannock Hill, on the hazelnut tree, hung Ragweed's earring. The earring's loop of metal was isolated enough, high enough, to draw lightning like a magnet.

With a great *crack!* a bolt of lightning shot from the clouds down toward the earring at enormous speed. When it struck, the earring's purple bead exploded into dust and its metal wire instantly vaporized into a shower of tiny sparks.

One solitary spark landed on a dry leaf. The leaf began

to smolder. When the smoldering leaf became hot enough, it burst into a small bud of flame.

And continued to burn.

A second leaf soon caught fire. . . . And then a third. And then a fourth . . . a tiny blaze in the dark night.

CHAPTER 12

Ereth Shares the Awful News

Ereth did not sleep much that night. He got up, he lay down, he turned around in circles, all the while wishing night would last forever. When day arrived, he would have to inform Poppy's family about what had happened to her. The mere thought of it made him moan. "Cauliflower Ca— No! No more swearing!" he cried. "Never again!"

Twice during the night, Ereth heard thunder rumble. Once, while squatting by the entryway to his log, he saw and heard a crack of lightning. Agitated, he listened for the sound of falling rain. None came. "Just lightning." He sighed. "No rain. No Poppy . . . only misery."

Through half-lidded eyes, the exhausted porcupine watched the eastern sky's gray glow proclaim the day's new dawn. As the light grew stronger, birds began to chirp their reedy songs. Rays of sunlight sliced through the forest like flaming swords. The long shadows cast by the forest's tall trees gradually withdrew, as if sliding back into their own roots. And slowly but with certainty, the morning heat proclaimed another scorching day.

Weary and tense, a panting Ereth closed his eyes. "I must tell them. Now."

He got up slowly, feeling a deep hunger. The only thing he had eaten the day before was a solitary dry twig. He searched his log but discovered nothing to eat. "Salt," he whimpered. "I need some salt!"

Having run out of excuses, the porcupine waddled out of his log. He blinked at the hot, bright sun and scanned the sky in search of clouds. Not one was in sight. "Bright is bad," said Ereth. "Night is nice. I don't have to look at anything." Then he muttered, "And no one can see me."

He gazed at Poppy's snag. Oh, how lovely it would be if his friend came strolling out as she had done so many times. She'd give a cheerful wave and cry, "Good morning, Ereth!" Perhaps she'd ask about him. Perhaps a tiny, damp kiss on his nose.

Ereth's vision became so blurry with tears he could almost see Poppy standing right in front of him. He closed his eyes.

"Good morning, Uncle Ereth!"

Ereth blinked open his eyes. There before him was Ragweed Junior. One of Junior's children was with him.

To Ereth, the youngster looked just like Junior.

Ereth glared at the mice. At that moment he *hated* Junior. Hated all mice who weren't his beloved friend!

"Hey, Uncle Ereth," said Junior. "This heat sure is something awful, isn't it? Did you catch that lightning last night? Came close. Maybe before the day is out we'll finally get some rain."

"I suppose . . . ," Ereth mumbled, only to retreat into silence.

"This is my son Spruce," Junior went on, bringing the young mouse forward. "I don't think you ever met him. Thought it was about time. Spruce, say hello to Uncle Ereth. He's Grandma Poppy's best friend. "

"'Lo," said Spruce, staring up in awe at the porcupine.

"Seems Spruce and Poppy have become great friends, too," said Junior. "He's bringing her a nut he found."

Spruce held up a half-eaten nut.

Ereth frowned.

"Is something the matter, Uncle Ereth?" said Junior. "You look like . . . you're in pain."

Suppressing a swear, Ereth said, "Why did you come here?"

"Like I said, we've come over to see Poppy. Thought we'd say hello to you, too."

"P-Poppy . . . ," Ereth stammered, "isn't here."

"Oh? She out?" asked Junior. "Gone off somewhere? Any idea where? When she'll be back?"

Ereth cleared his throat. "Last time I saw her," he said, "she . . . she was . . . d—" He could not get the fatal word out. Instead he said, "She was flying."

Spruce stared at Ereth and then turned to look up at his father. "Dad, did . . . Uncle Ereth say Grandma was . . . flying?"

Junior did not seem to hear his son's question. To Ereth he said, "My mom was . . . *what*?"

"Flying."

"*Flying?* Where?"

"In the sky!" snapped Ereth. "Where else would she fly?"

Junior gazed at the porcupine. "Uncle Ereth," he said after a moment, "has the heat gotten to you? It makes some dizzy. Confused. Especially old guys."

"I am *not* old!" Ereth barked.

The force of Ereth's words made Spruce back up a step and press against his father, but he never took his eyes off the porcupine.

"No, of course not," said Junior. "Sorry. I shouldn't have said that. Well, I guess Spruce and I had better get going. Come on, pal." The two mice moved toward Poppy's snag.

Spruce, staying close to his father, kept glancing back over his shoulder at Ereth, a perplexed look on his face.

"I'm telling you!" Ereth cried after them. "She's not there."

"That's okay," Junior called back. "We'll just check for ourselves."

"Maybe she is there," Ereth whispered under his breath. He allowed himself a stirring of hope.

He watched closely as Junior and Spruce went inside the snag. He was still looking when, a few moments later, the two came back out, alone. As the mice returned to him, Ereth glanced away.

"Guess you're right, Uncle Ereth," said Junior. "She's not there. Doesn't look like she packed up, either. Must have gone in a hurry because things were just left about. Really, have you any idea where Poppy went or . . . or when she might be coming back?"

"How many times do I have to tell you?" said Ereth. "The . . . last time I saw her . . . she was . . . she was flying straight up into the sky."

"Dad," Spruce whispered, loud enough for Ereth to hear, "I think he really did say that Grandma Poppy was flying."

"Yes!" bellowed Ereth. "That's what I said!"

"Uncle Ereth, please, you don't have to yell. Just explain yourself."

Ereth gulped a draught of hot air, then said, "Yesterday I went down to Glitter Creek to take a bath but instead I almost drowned in the mud and called for help, so of course Poppy came and helped *me*—*she* cares for me—which I was grateful for except the next thing I knew she was gone. Vanished. Then I saw something that looked like her flying straight up in the air. Which is to say I'm pretty sure I did see her . . ." Ereth faltered.

Junior's whiskers trembled visibly. "Saw . . . *what?*"

"Poppy's . . . ghost," said Ereth, barely whispering.

"Her . . . *ghost?*" exclaimed Junior.

"Yes!" screamed Ereth at the top of his voice. "Poppy's *ghost!*"

"Are you trying to tell me" said Junior, "that Poppy's . . . ghost went flying into the sky, which would mean that she must have . . . ?"

"Died!" yelled the porcupine. "Yes! Died saving me! Who else would she have died for?"

Junior stared up at the porcupine. "Mom? *Dead?*"

Ereth looked everywhere except at Junior.

Spruce broke the heavy silence that followed. "Dad," he whispered, "is Uncle Ereth saying Grandma Poppy . . . *died?*"

"Shhh!" Junior said gently. But to Ereth he spoke with some severity. "Uncle Ereth, *is* that what you're saying?"

"Yes!" cried Ereth. "Yes, yes, yes!"

"I . . . I can't believe it," stammered Junior.

"Dad, how could Grandma be dead?" interjected Spruce. "I just met her."

"Then how else," said Ereth, still gasping from the effort of his long explanation, "can you explain the fact that I saw her ghost soaring up into the sky?"

"But where . . . when . . . how?" Junior continued to stammer.

Trying to keep from bursting into tears, Ereth slowly repeated the events of his trip to Glitter Creek.

"Uncle Ereth," said Junior, now speaking in a soft, pleading voice, "are you . . . absolutely certain . . . you saw Poppy's . . . *ghost?*"

"How many times must I say *yes?*" cried Ereth.

Junior turned to Spruce. "Spruce," he said. "I think we need to go." To Ereth he said, "I'll check Poppy's snag again more thoroughly and see if she left some kind of message." Not waiting for a reply, he turned and led Spruce away.

Ereth watched them go. Then he gazed up at the sky, as if Poppy might be there. The sky was blue and cloudless, and the air so hot it seemed to quiver before his eyes. He felt dizzy. Sick. Miserable. The whole world—including

him—was turning old. Drying up! He swished his tail and ground his teeth. He wanted to bite something or somebody. To swear. All he did in the end, however, was to turn slowly about and make his way into the deep, dark end of his log. There he hunkered down, trying desperately to understand what he should do.

"I need to make everyone know how much I cared for Poppy," he whispered at last. "I'm the only one who really knew and understood her. The only one who truly loved her. How am I going to show that?" He thought hard. "I know! A funeral service! That's what I'll do for her. Yes! The biggest, best, most beautiful funeral service this forest has ever seen."

"Uncle Ereth?"

With a start, Ereth looked up. Spruce had come into the log. The young mouse held a paw to his nose.

"What's the matter with your nose?" Ereth demanded.

Spruce said, "It stinks in here."

"Never mind stinks," Ereth snapped. "Did you find anything about Poppy?"

"Dad is still looking," said Spruce. "Uncle Ereth, do you really, really think Grandma Poppy was flying?"

"Her ghost was."

"Then I think she's fine," said Spruce.

"How could she be fine?" demanded Ereth, quite sure

this was the most irritating mouse he had ever met.

Before Spruce could reply, Junior came into the log. "I'm afraid you must be right, Uncle Ereth. Not one sign of her." He sighed. "I'll need to tell my brothers and sisters. The rest of the family too."

"Good idea," said Ereth, relieved that he would not have to do the task. Junior turned to go.

"Hold it!" cried Ereth.

Junior and Spruce stopped.

"What about a funeral service?"

"I guess," said Junior, "but . . ."

"Your family will want something," insisted the porcupine. "The whole family could gather. Pay their respects."

"Well, *if* what you say is true, but—"

"It is true!" said Ereth with something like anger. "I'll organize it."

"Uncle Ereth, I need to check some more. But I'm sure it would be kind of you. You were her best friend. And if Poppy really . . . died . . . I'm sure the whole family would appreciate it."

"I'll give a speech about her."

"Sure. Something short," said Junior. "I imagine my brothers and sisters will want to speak too. Uncle Ereth, could you truly arrange things?"

"Of course," muttered Ereth.

"Thank you," said Junior. He went out of the log, Spruce by his side.

As the two mice left the log, Ereth heard the youngster say, "Don't worry, Dad. I'm going to find her."

Alone again, Ereth snorted, "'*Something short*'! I'll show them what a best friend can do. I'll show them a funeral that no one will ever forget!"

Next moment Ereth became quiet. Then he said, "Of course if Poppy hadn't died, I wouldn't have to do any of this! She should have known how much I dislike making speeches. Lazy creature! If *I* died, I'd be making my own speech!"

CHAPTER 13

The Bat Cave

POPPY WOKE SLOWLY, trying to understand why she was so cold. *Has the heat wave* finally *broken?* She opened her eyes. *Why is it so dim? Where am I?*

Next moment she recalled everything that had happened the day before: spending time with Spruce; visiting Bannock Hill; saving Ereth; being catapulted into the sky; Luci, the young bat, catching her; flying into a cave. And now here she was.

She sat up and stretched. Licking her paws, she washed her face, starting with her nose and ending with her ears, inside and out. Only then did she really look about, sniff the cold air, and listen.

Unlike when she'd entered the cave, it was no longer completely dark. A beam of light burst through the high, jagged rock wall so that Poppy could see a little. As she looked on, the light steadily increased, becoming brighter and broader: the rising sun shining through a high hole. The light cast a soft golden glow that illuminated most of the cave.

"Oh my!" Poppy exclaimed. For what she now saw was a vast, vaulted, irregularly shaped open space with countless nooks, crannies and cracks, steep rock walls, a rough and pebbly floor, and a ceiling mostly shrouded in darkness. From the ceiling hung stone cones, some small, others huge. Thrusting up from the floor of the cave were just as many cones. Some of these cones—above and below—met and stood ground to roof, like lopsided pillars.

As the light grew brighter, Poppy noticed other shapes: a cluster of berries, not edible ones such as she knew but more curious stone formations. Overhead, long stone ribbons were arrayed like partially dropped curtains. In two other places Poppy saw what appeared to be delicately intertwined threads—like loosely woven birds' nests—but, again, made of stone. The stone, shining in various tints of gold, seemed alive and flowing, changing form as the light shifted.

"How magical!" Poppy whispered. "How wonderfully strange. I never could have even imagined such a place! I'm *so* lucky to see it!"

Aware now that she was standing on something like a stone platform a few inches off the ground, Poppy crawled down upon the cave's cold, hard floor and moved in and about the stone teeth. She soon came upon a small pool of clear water noiselessly bubbling up from below.

She took a sip and found it cold and sweet. But while the water quenched her thirst, it reminded her how hungry she was. Her stomach gurgled.

She looked about. As beautiful as the cave was, there appeared to be nothing growing or, for that matter, even alive—except her. And the silence! It was the deepest, purest silence she had ever heard—as if the whole world was holding its breath.

Poppy wondered where Luci was. She assumed the bats were somewhere near. She shuddered a little at the thought.

Poppy looked up at the beam of sunlight again. As she watched, the light gradually shifted its angle downward—an indication that the sun was just rising. Poppy supposed the light was coming from the same hole Luci had used to enter the cave. That gave her an idea: if she had arrived through that hole, surely she should be able to leave the same way.

As Poppy considered the hole, she began to think about her family. They might be wondering where she was. Ereth,

too, of course, though she did not think the grouchy porcupine would worry much about her.

And the cold was really bothering her. While it would be fastest to persuade Luci to take her home, Poppy asked herself if she really wanted to *fly* back. Luci *was* just a beginner, and the young bat had said Poppy was heavy. *What if she dropped me?* thought Poppy.

No, best to do it on her own. *That's always been my way of doing things,* she told herself. The thought gave her strength.

Poppy scrutinized the wall until she spotted a zigzag path leading from the floor of the cave up to the entry hole. When she drew closer, she saw that the path was actually a small ledge on the stone wall's face. It required very little

effort to climb onto it. Though the ledge was narrow and rough, Poppy was able to move along with ease until she stood several feet above the floor of the cave. There the path ended.

She had reached the first of the many zigzags that she had previously noticed. Another ledge, a little higher, cut back in the other direction. It would take her farther along.

Standing on tiptoes and pressing her plump belly against the cold stone, Poppy extended one paw up as far as possible, and then grasped the edge of the higher ledge. It crumbled, bringing a small shower of pebbles onto her head. A second try was successful.

Tightly grasping the ledge, Poppy pulled herself up so

that she was dangling from one paw. She reached up with another paw. Hanging by two paws now, she summoned all her strength and, pushing with her rear legs, pulled herself to the next higher ledge.

Panting hard, but safe on this third ledge, Poppy sat, rested, and caught her breath.

Once refreshed, Poppy moved on, going upward at a steep angle. She glanced at the beam of light. It was now pointing down, a sure indication that the sun was higher in the sky. It must be midmorning. As the day progressed, the cave would eventually become dim and then dark. If Poppy knew one thing, it was that she did *not* want to climb in the dark.

She hurried along the ledge. It narrowed, but it took her a good way up before coming to an end.

Poppy looked down only to discover that she was much higher than she had thought. The pointy rocks below no longer seemed beautiful, but menacing.

A tremor of nervousness swept through her. "It's a good thing I'm going up," she told herself, "because I won't be able to get down."

Unless I fall.

Poppy began to tremble so much she had to sit. "Foolish mouse," she scolded herself. "Coming up here was not smart. I need to accept that I simply cannot do everything

I want anymore. At least, not alone."

She licked her lips. Her tail and whiskers twitched. She felt cold. She made up her mind not to look down. Or back. Or anywhere but up.

Forcing herself to stand, she stole a glance up toward the hole. It still seemed very far. Not that there was a choice. She had to continue going higher—except it now felt as if she had a very long way to go. The realization made her feel tense.

Taking a deep breath to calm herself, Poppy reached up and wedged her paw into a small crevice. The rock pinched, but her paw held. Using her rear toes to push into the rock, she lifted another paw and searched for a crevice higher than the first. Not finding one, Poppy glanced up—only to slip a little. Her heart pounded. To steady herself, she pressed her body against the rock.

Not daring to look, Poppy again reached higher and searched with her paw for another hold. After much fumbling, she located a small crack, gripped it, and pulled.

Though higher up, the climb was beginning to make her feel dizzy. Still, Poppy knew she had to continue on. Which she did. Slowly. Painfully.

Then, like a bubble bursting, Poppy's strength collapsed. She could not go up any higher. All she could do was cling to the cold rock. As she hung there, suspended, her paws began to ache. A painful cramp seized one of her legs.

Her grip weakened. She started to slip. A frantic snatch at the rock proved useless. The rock gave way. Poppy began to drop.

"Help!" Poppy screamed as she plummeted toward the rock teeth below. "Help!"

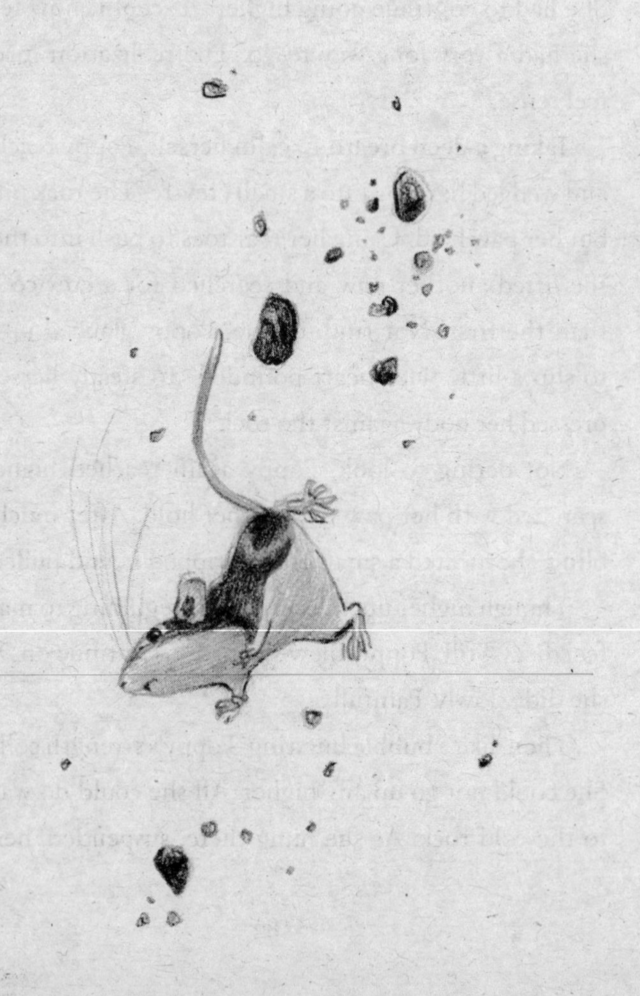

CHAPTER 14

Poppy and Luci

As Poppy plunged, she felt a sharp pinch on her back. She was no longer falling. Gasping for breath, heart pounding, she twisted around and looked up. Luci was holding her.

"Miss Poppy," said Luci, "are you sure you can't fly?"

"Really, I . . . can't," Poppy managed.

"Then how come I keep finding you up in the air?" asked Luci. "I mean, how do you *get* there?"

"I was going up but then fell," Poppy explained.

"No offense, Miss Poppy, but Mom is always saying, 'Luci, always decide which direction you want to go—up or down.'"

Poppy sighed. "I'd like to go down."

"Okay," said Luci. The bat glided down to the floor of the cave and set Poppy loose.

Poppy stood up on weak hind legs and looked about. The light was softer now, and Luci was nowhere to be seen.

"Luci?" Poppy called.

"Over here."

Poppy turned. Luci was hanging upside down from one of the stone cones.

"What I don't understand," said the bat as if hanging upside down was a perfectly normal way to have a conversation, "is, if you can't fly, how did you manage to get up so high on the wall?"

"I climbed."

"*Climbed!* Why would you ever do that?"

"I was trying to go home," Poppy admitted, slightly embarrassed.

"Please don't go home yet," said Luci. "I told everybody about you. They really want to meet you. We *never* have visitors. Would you be willing to meet some of them before you go?"

"Can I walk?" Poppy asked, greatly comforted that Luci had at least acknowledged that she would be leaving.

"Much better to fly."

"What time is it?"

"Almost noon," said Luci.

"Promise not to drop me?"

Luci giggled. "Miss Poppy, no offense, but you're the one who keeps falling."

"All right then," said Poppy.

Luci spread her wings, dropped down, gently pinched Poppy's furry back, and lifted the mouse into the air. In moments, the two were flying through the cave.

Now Poppy could see that the cave was much bigger than she had imagined, filled as it was with endlessly strange shapes and formations. It also extended in countless directions, like the branches of a tree. Luci, however, seemed to know exactly where she was going. She swooped, turned, and entered a dark tunnel, emerging at the other end into a spectacular space: a great domed area with golden arrows of light streaming down from above.

The beams shone on an almost perfectly round lake, its blue-green surface eerily translucent and surrounded by a

beach of what appeared to be white sand.

"Where does that light come from?" Poppy asked.

"Small holes in the cave roof," replied Luci. "Oldwing says this place used to be a volcano."

"Who's Oldwing?"

"Our leader. Anyway, we can fly in and out up there, but it's easier to use that big entryway."

"Where do you all stay?" asked Poppy.

"Look around!" cried Luci.

Poppy looked and saw that the walls of the cave were covered with bats huddled together upside down, clinging to the walls. She could hear a multitude of squeaks and rustling noises.

"Welcome to my home," said Luci, as she glided down to the beach.

"Is this sand?" Poppy asked.

"Salt," said Luci.

"Salt!" *I must tell Ereth,* thought Poppy, only to be distracted by a great fluff and flutter of leathery wings as a large number of bats dropped down all around her. As they landed, they drew their wings up to their ears and hunched over, their beady-bright eyes focused on Poppy.

Like Luci, these bats were covered with brown fur. They had stub noses on flat, dour faces and large, pointy, twitching ears.

Wanting to show her good manners and friendly intentions, Poppy sat up on her hind legs, smiled, took a deep breath, and, in her most cheerful voice, said, "Hi! My name is Poppy. I'm a deer mouse. I live in Dimwood Forest."

The bats stared at her with their bright eyes. Now and again ears flicked, and occasionally one of them opened a mouth, as if yawning. That's when Poppy noticed the bats' teeth—and how sharp they were.

CHAPTER 15

On Bannock Hill

BY MORNING a few leaves on the Bannock Hill hazelnut tree were burning steadily. It was enough flame to cause the thin branch upon which the leaves had grown to catch fire.

The small flame continued to burn, moving along the branch like a long, slow fuse, moving—by midday—ever closer to the trunk of the tree.

CHAPTER 16

Spruce

As Spruce and Junior walked slowly from Ereth's log toward their own underground home, the young mouse kept looking up at his father's sad face, then turning back to consider the porcupine. After a while Spruce said, "Dad—"

"Spruce," said Junior, his voice low, "please be quiet. I have a lot to think about."

"But, Dad, I need to say something."

Junior stopped. "Spruce, we just heard some very disturbing news about Grandma Poppy. I am trying to—"

"But, Dad," Spruce interrupted. "I know why Grandma Poppy was flying."

"What are you talking about?"

"Yesterday Grandma and I went for a walk. First we looked for foxes. Then—"

"Are you telling me you and Poppy went *looking* for a fox?"

"Yup."

"Spruce . . . do you know how you often make up stories, and how exaggerated they are?"

"But—"

"As we've told you many times, it's really not a good habit."

"No, listen, Dad. Grandma said a mouse has to do what a mouse has to do."

Junior sighed. "Where did she get that notion?"

"Your uncle Ragweed."

Junior shook his head. "Spruce, you don't know anything about him."

"I do, too. Because I look like him," continued Spruce. "But see, Grandma Poppy wanted to *do* something, so I bet she decided to learn to fly, and—"

"Spruce," Junior cut in, "what Uncle Ereth said was that Poppy . . . died."

"But, Dad!" cried Spruce.

"Spruce, let's just get home."

When they reached the entryway to their underground home, Junior paused. "Now, Spruce, I have to talk to your mother. Alone. But I want you to promise me something."

"Okay."

"Please, do *not* tell your brothers and sisters that Grandma Poppy died. *If* it is true, I need to explain things my way—not yours. Can you promise me?"

"But, Dad, I really think Grandma got lost because—"

"Spruce! Just do as I ask: do *not* tell your brothers and sisters Grandma Poppy died."

"Okay, because she—"

"Thank you!"

Junior led the way into the hole, where he gave Spruce

a hasty nuzzle and then went down the main tunnel in search of Laurel. "Remember what you promised!" he called back.

"All she did was fly," Spruce muttered to himself. "And she got lost because she's so old."

The young mouse went into the children's den, where he found his brother Lodgepole rolling mud balls and piling them up into a pyramid. For a moment Spruce just watched. Compared to Grandma Poppy's flying, making mud balls seemed pretty dull.

"Guess what?" Spruce announced.

"What?" said Lodgepole, not turning away from his work.

"Grandma Poppy learned to fly."

Lodgepole looked at his brother. "Yesterday you said you and Grandma Poppy were looking for a fox."

"We were."

"Mice don't go looking for foxes," said Lodgepole before turning back to his mud balls. "And mice can't fly."

"Grandma Poppy did," insisted Spruce. "I'm not making it up. Uncle Ereth saw her flying. Only she got lost."

Lodgepole looked at his brother again. "Why would Grandma Poppy fly?"

"A mouse has to do what a mouse has to do."

"What's that supposed to mean?"

Instead of answering, Spruce said, "I'm calling a meeting. Get everybody together."

"What for?"

"We have to find Grandma Poppy."

Twenty minutes later, Spruce had managed to collect only three of his siblings: his brothers Lodgepole and Dogbane and his sister Clover.

Spruce repeated what he had told Lodgepole about Poppy. "See, she just learned to fly, but Grandma Poppy is real old so she got lost."

"When you're old," agreed Clover, "you shouldn't go anywhere far."

"Actually," said Lodgepole, "we're young and we don't go far either."

"Listen to me!" cried Spruce. "We have to find her!"

"Spruce," said Lodgepole, "everybody knows you make up stories."

"Because you're the runt of the family," added Clover, giving him a push.

"I'm *not* making this up!" cried Spruce, pushing back. "Uncle Ereth saw her flying."

"I met him," said Dogbane. "He's old, too."

"Yeah," added Lodgepole. "And he smells."

"We have to find Grandma," Spruce insisted. "And we should start looking by Glitter Creek."

"Shouldn't we tell Mom and Dad we're going?" asked Dogbane.

"If you do," said Spruce, "it won't be a surprise when we bring Grandma home. What kind of fun will that be?"

"I don't care about the fun," said Clover. "I just think we should tell them where we're going."

"But Spruce is right," said Dogbane. "It would be cool to find Grandma and bring her home."

"She'd really like it if we found her," Spruce insisted. "But if none of you want to come, too bad. I'm going myself." He marched off.

The three remaining young mice looked at one another. "How come Spruce always thinks he knows everything?" said Clover.

"Ma says he's a small mouse with a large imagination," said Lodgepole.

"Maybe this time he's right," said Dogbane, and he followed Spruce.

Lodgepole and Clover remained. "They're going to get into trouble," predicted Clover.

Lodgepole turned back to his mud balls. "Big trouble."

CHAPTER 17

Ereth Chooses

ERETH DECIDED Poppy's funeral service had to be in the perfect place. Large enough to hold her whole family. More importantly, it needed to be where each of them could see and hear what he had to say.

After much hard thinking, he recalled a secluded dell open to the sky yet surrounded by trees. He remembered it as being carpeted with green grass and clover. Butterflies and bees floated about, along with the occasional dragonfly, flashing its rainbow-tinted wings in the air. The morning's sun would warm the grass dew into mist, turning the dell into a bowl of sweet perfume. By noon, every white, blue, and yellow flower would unfold. Twilight always transformed the dell into a world of softness.

But when Ereth reached the dell, he found it blighted by the summer's drought. The grass was brown. Withered leaves hung from the encircling trees. Not a solitary flower was in sight. No insects flittered about, except for the odd leaping grasshopper, its wings clacking angrily in the swollen heat.

Still, Ereth was convinced the dell was the best spot. The beaten-down grass would actually make it easier for the small mice to see him. At twilight it would be cooler.

He selected a boulder along the dell's upper edge from which to speak. It was flat and easy for him to climb. All of Poppy's family would be able to see him. "Just as it should be," he mumbled.

Ereth stepped to the edge of the boulder, sat up on his hind legs, and looked out over the dell.

"My friends!" he began. "My full name is Erethizon Dorsatum, and for those younger folk before me who may be ignorant as to *what* I am, I am a porcupine. So if you don't pay attention, you'll get a quill up the snoot!

"I'm here today," he said, "to speak about my dear friend, Poppy, unhappily now passed . . . up. It's a sad occasion. So let me begin by—"

Ereth stopped speaking. "I can't stand this!" he shouted to no one. Tears filled his eyes and dripped off the end of his nose. He could barely talk or breathe. Instead, he bent down and wiped his eyes and nose with his front paws. "I did love Poppy," he whispered. "I really did. I know I didn't do it well, but I did love her. And I . . . miss her so much! What else is there to say? Poppy's gone. That's all that matters."

His tears continued to fall. He ceased speaking. Even the grasshoppers were still.

CHAPTER 18

Spruce Goes Looking for Poppy

SPRUCE CRAWLED out of the family's underground home and looked about the dry forest. There were two paths he could take. Having never traveled to Glitter Creek on his own, he was not sure which one to choose.

As the young mouse tried to make up his mind, Dogbane popped out of the entryway. "Okay," he announced. "I'll come with you."

"Anyone else?" asked Spruce.

"Just me," said Dogbane. "And since this is your idea, you'd better know the right way to the creek. Or were you just pretending?"

"I'm pretty sure it's this way," said Spruce, making a quick guess and starting down one of the paths. "You coming?"

Dogbane held back. "*Pretty* sure or *very* sure?"

"You scared to come?" said Spruce, half hoping his brother would say yes so he could go alone. It would be so neat to be the one to discover where Grandma Poppy had landed.

"Not me," said Dogbane. He hurried after Spruce.

The brothers went along the path for a while without speaking. After a few minutes Dogbane sat down in a pool of shade by the side of the path. "It's too hot to go fast," he announced.

Spruce joined him. He stared up at the trees. He was used to going off alone, but today the trees seemed taller than he had remembered them.

Dogbane followed his gaze. "How high do you think those trees are?"

"Ten miles," said Spruce, blurting out the first thing that came into his head.

Dogbane looked at his brother. "That's not true."

"Is," insisted Spruce.

"Then how far is it till we get to the creek?" Dogbane asked.

"Thirty miles."

"*Thirty miles!*" cried Dogbane. "How long is this walk going to take?"

"Twelve minutes," said Spruce.

Dogbane considered. "How many minutes have we been going?"

"Six."

"Come on," said Dogbane. "Admit it, you just make up this stuff. You don't know what you're doing."

"Do," said Spruce.

"And is this really, *really* the way to the creek?"

"Don't believe me if you don't want to."

"And you're sure Grandma Poppy is at the creek?"

"That's where Uncle Ereth saw her."

Dogbane sighed. "Fine. Let's keep moving."

The two mice continued along the path. Ten minutes later Dogbane halted. "How close to the creek are we now?"

Spruce studied the path. A little hill rose up before them. "See that hill?" he said. "From the top you'll be able to see the creek."

"Fine."

They went on and soon reached the top of the hill. Instead of seeing Glitter Creek, they arrived at a fork in the path.

"You said Glitter Creek would be here," said Dogbane.

"I said," insisted Spruce, "we'd see the path that led to the creek."

"You did not."

"Did!"

"Fine! Which path do we take?"

Spruce considered. There was nothing to distinguish

one path from the other. He turned and stole a glance back over the way they had come, and wondered if, after all, it might be better to go home.

"Know what?" said Dogbane. "You really don't know what you're talking about."

"I do, too."

"This is just stupid," said Dogbane. "Grandma is fine. Mice can't fly. I'm going home."

"I don't scare so easy," said Spruce, and he walked ahead, taking the path that led to the right.

Dogbane watched him go. "Runt!" he shouted, then spun around and began to run toward home.

Spruce kept going. But after a few moments, he stopped and glanced around. "Dogbane!" he cried. "I'm going!"

No reply came. Uneasy, Spruce reminded himself what Grandma Poppy had told him: *"A mouse has to do what a mouse has to do."* According to Grandma, a mouse named Ragweed said that. Since Spruce's father was also named Ragweed he supposed his father would say the same thing. *Well, so should he.*

Spruce gazed down the path he had chosen to get to the creek: he would do it alone.

As Spruce walked on, he thought: *A mouse has to do . . . But it would be a lot easier to find Grandma if I knew where she landed.*

CHAPTER 19

Poppy and the Bats

DEEP WITHIN THE BAT CAVE, Poppy gazed about at the bats that surrounded her. Bent over, wings folded up to their ears, they returned her scrutiny with solemn silence. If there was a smile on any bat face, Poppy did not see it.

There was some nervous shuffling among the bats, but not a word was spoken. Then one bat crawled forward. His large leathery wings were hunched up to his pointy ears, and he waddled with slow, forceful, jerky movements. There was gray about his snout, his flaring nostrils were hairy, and his black eyes were surrounded with wrinkles. Poppy felt inclined to retreat, but she had no place to go.

"Miss Poppy," said the bat, speaking slowly in a high, cracking voice. "I am called Oldwing by my family. On their behalf I extend a welcome.

"Being the oldest bat in this community," he continued, "I have the privilege to receive you in our domain. Our inquisitiveness is equaled only by our timidity. It's unusual for us to receive visitors. Indeed, we have never seen the likes of you here before. You say you are a deer mouse."

Poppy nodded. "I am, though Luci thought I was a moth."

Her remark brought a few broad, toothy grins, some nodding, and a few squeaks that sounded like giggles.

"Though it was a mistake," said Poppy, relaxing a bit, "my visit has been quite wonderful. It's not often I have such new experiences. Your cave is . . . very beautiful."

"Thank you," returned Oldwing with a slight folding and unfolding of his wings.

"But why don't you have visitors?" asked Poppy. "I'm sure others would like to see your home."

"Few know how to enter this cave," said Oldwing.

"You mean you have to fly in."

"There is another way," said Oldwing. "But we prefer to keep it secret. No, there's a more important reason we have few visitors."

Oldwing closed his eyes. "Miss Poppy," the bat said, speaking with care as he opened his eyes, "the truth is, we bats are not considered good company. Many think we are full of disease. That we are aggressive. Dangerous. Ugly. Blind as a bat, as others say. Some go so far as to consider us evil. None of these things are true. Even so, bats are feared and, being feared, scorned."

Poppy, recalling her earlier thoughts about bats, felt embarrassed.

"Miss Poppy," Oldwing continued, "the truth is, we are a close-knit family who offer no harm to anybody. When you return to your home, you will do us a great kindness if you educate your family and friends as to the truth about us."

"I certainly will," said Poppy, cheered by the idea that it was understood she would be going home.

"On behalf of my family, I thank you," said Oldwing, nodding. "I hope you will call on us if we can ever be of assistance. For now, please stay as long as you desire."

"That's very kind," said Poppy. "But I've been gone from my family a long time. They're probably worried. Besides, Luci tells me you don't have the kind of food I eat."

"What food is that?" asked Oldwing.

"Seeds, mostly," said Poppy.

"Alas," said the bat, "Luci is correct. But please, do come again. Bring your family. We have plenty of room. For now, Luci can take you home."

"Thank you," said Poppy. "You've been so pleasant. This is a strange and wonderful world. Being old, I'm glad to have seen it at my age."

Oldwing nodded. "Being old brings wisdom, but not

always the strength to use it."

"Well," said Poppy, "I suppose we can still try, can't we?"

"Indeed," said Oldwing, "as my great-great-grandfather Longwing once said, 'To try is to be young.' Perhaps, Miss Poppy, you are not as old as you think. Until next time, farewell."

Next moment, there was a great rush and whirl of leathery wings as the bats rose in the air. Though crowded and close, none bumped. As Poppy watched, the bats flew high into the dome of the cave and then attached themselves to the wall in a great, crowded mass.

"Oh my," said a voice behind Poppy, "isn't Oldwing sweet? We all love him to bits."

Poppy turned. Luci had remained. "He was kind," said Poppy. "Luci, can I really go home now?"

"Sure," said Luci. "My ma said I could take you this evening."

"Is there any way I could go now, on my own?"

"Well," Luci whispered. "You heard what Oldwing said. We have another way. But you'd have to"—she grimaced—"*crawl.*"

"Please, Luci," Poppy pleaded. "I truly need to get home. I'm used to crawling, and it's very cold in here for me. Besides, I'm really hungry. I haven't eaten for a whole day."

"Do you promise not to tell?"

"Of course," said Poppy.

"I'd have to fly you a little bit."

"That's fine," Poppy coaxed.

"I suppose it is my fault you're here," said Luci.

"Luci, I truly enjoyed myself," Poppy replied.

Luci grinned. "Let's do it."

Poppy lay down to make it easier for Luci to pick her up. Soon they were flying through the cave, following a series of sharp twists and turns until Luci set Poppy into a corner in front of what appeared, in the murky gloom, to be a tunnel.

"There it is," Luci whispered. "The way Oldwing mentioned. I never used it myself. They say you just go right on through. From the other end you should be able to find your way out to the forest."

"Thank you," said Poppy, eyeing the tunnel entryway with dismay. Its darkness was not inviting.

"Miss Poppy," said Lucy, "I'm still mortified I thought you were a moth."

"Never mind," said Poppy. "It's been a good change for an old mouse."

"Miss Poppy, you don't act *old*," said Luci. "And I'd really like to see you again. Just give a call at twilight when we're out flying. The higher your voice, the more likely I'll hear. See you later, moth-mouse!" she cried, and with a flutter of

her leathery wings, Luci took off.

"Good-bye!" Poppy called after her. For a few moments, she watched as the young bat disappeared into the gloomy, dim recesses of the cave.

Alone, Poppy turned and faced the tunnel. Its entry was round, its floor strewn with countless stones, large and small, and it was much darker than she would have wished. She reminded herself that she really wanted to get home, wanted to see the sun, wanted to eat.

"Oh well," said Poppy, "sometimes an old mouse still has to do what a young mouse has to do," and she stepped into the tunnel.

CHAPTER 20

Poppy in the Tunnel

THE FARTHER POPPY WENT into the tunnel, the darker it became. Once, twice, she looked back over her shoulder. When she looked a third time, the entryway was no longer visible, no lighter than when Poppy had first entered the bat cave. Though this made her hesitate, she reminded herself that it was the best way to get home, and she continued on, feeling her way through the darkness with her front paws.

As Poppy crept forward, she pitched her ears ahead and wiggled her nose to catch any sound or smell that might alert her to trouble. At first there was nothing to alarm her. Then she heard a tiny sound.

Stopping immediately, Poppy became extra alert. She listened, sniffed, and stared into the darkness. The sound repeated itself, but so tantalizingly brief and faint, it was impossible to identify. She inched forward. Within moments the noise came again, and this time Poppy knew she had detected the steady breathing of a sleeping animal.

Though apprehensive, she continued to creep forward, paused, and stuck up her nose. A gentle flow of air suggested that the end of the tunnel was not too far. But mingled in that same breeze between her and the outside was the scent of an animal.

Wondering if it would be best to retreat and ask Luci to fly her home, Poppy peered back into the darkness. She reminded herself that there was no certainty she'd be able to find her young friend. Besides, she was very hungry and there was no food in the cave. *Maybe,* she thought, *the animal ahead is no one I need worry about.*

She would have to see for herself.

Taking a deep breath, Poppy continued forward with extreme caution. Every few steps she paused to look, listen, and smell.

When a faint light bloomed ahead, Poppy halted. The cave entrance must be really close. Just the thought gave her new energy. Though she wanted to race forward and dance in the sunlight, she held back. The breathing sound was still there. *Be cautious!* all her instincts insisted. *Be very cautious.*

She went on. Her whiskers soon detected a stronger flow of warm air coming in her direction, and the breathing sound grew even louder. She was getting closer.

Poppy sat up on her hind legs, lifted her nose, and took a deep breath. She had no doubt: it was the scent of a large animal. But what *kind* of animal? Friendly? Unfriendly? Indifferent to mice or not? Impossible to tell. Another

sniff. The scent was oddly familiar, teasingly vague. But who was it? She could not place it.

She continued to creep forward. The farther she went, the more the light grew until she no longer had to feel her way. She could see.

Poppy approached a sharp bend in the tunnel. Though she would have liked to bolt forward, she took a careful peek around the corner. After so much darkness, the glare of the bright sunlight blinded her momentarily. Blinking, she drew back, rubbed her eyes with her paws, and took another look. Once Poppy adjusted to the brightness, she could see the entryway as well as bushes beyond. And just inside the entryway lay a large animal curled up in a ball.

To her disgust and horror, she also saw the scattered remains of bones, remnants of small creatures—like herself—that this monster presumably had eaten.

As Poppy scrutinized the animal, its ears—long and pointy—perked up and twitched. Then the creature rearranged itself, shifted about, and briefly waved a long, bushy red tail. Its claws extended, then retracted. With its eyes closed, the animal lifted its head, revealing a long, delicately pointed nose replete with black whiskers. Finally, it gave a wide yawn, showing many sharp teeth, then lowered its head and curled up into a ball again.

By then Poppy knew exactly who it was: Bounder the fox.

CHAPTER 21

The Fire

THE BRANCH on the Bannock Hill hazelnut tree continued to burn, the flame moving steadily until it reached the dry trunk of the tree. Fed by more fuel, the fire burned brighter and hotter. It burned up, and it burned down. As it burned, a thin ribbon of dark smoke rose into the sky.

The fire soon reached the ground, setting aflame the brittle dry grasses and dead leaves that lay close by.

Before long, the entire crown of Bannock Hill was smoldering, creating a dark cloud of smoke and making the air even hazier than it already had been.

When a gentle burst of wind touched the hilltop, the whole summit exploded into flames. As the fire's intensity increased, it began to spread down the hill in the direction of Tar Road and the wooden bridge over Glitter Creek.

Beyond the creek lay Dimwood Forest.

CHAPTER 22

Ereth Looks at Himself

ERETH CROUCHED in the deepest, darkest part of his hollow log. Now and again he gnawed noisily on an old, dry twig. Finding it tasteless, he stopped often only to start again when he could think of nothing else to do.

"I suppose it has to be me who plans Poppy's funeral," he grumbled. "Nobody else offered. Nobody else could. How typical. They leave everything to me. What would Dimwood Forest be without me? Trees!"

The porcupine closed his eyes, shifted his prickly bulk, and twitched his tail until his quills rattled.

"What's important," he declared, "is that it be a dignified funeral. All about Poppy. So everyone will learn what a wonderful creature she was. Nobody like her in the whole forest. No one. Not even . . . me."

He closed his eyes and tried to remember how—it

seemed so long ago—he had first met Poppy. Ah, yes! It was a fox, named Bounder, who had chased her into his log. "Funny how that happened," Ereth mused. "Silly mouse! Poppy thought I was going to eat her. As if I'd eat meat. Yuck! Meat is disgusting."

Then Ereth thought about all the things he should have said to Poppy when she was alive. "There never was any time," he whispered. "How could I say the things I should have said if she didn't let me say them? She was always so busy. I never expected she would just fly off the way she did. Not bothering to say good-bye. Just . . . poof! Gone! Not very polite."

The more Ereth thought about Poppy, the more agitated he became until, unable to stay still, he heaved himself up and waddled out of his log. "I mustn't think about her anymore," he said. "It's making me crazy. Anyway, it's about time I started to think of myself."

Even so, he was unable to keep himself from trudging up to Poppy's snag, staring at it bleakly, shaking his head in dismay, and then turning to lumber into the woods.

As Ereth went along, he grumbled about his aching muscles, bad food, the lack of salt, and the air, which was hot, thick as glue and just as sticky. He felt heavy, and itchy.

Surely this was the hottest day of all, so hot even the forest insects were silent. He was convinced that he was the

sole creature moving, for the only sounds he heard were his own footsteps on the parched grass. The sound—scratchy and crunchy—irritated him.

"With Poppy gone, nothing is good!" he muttered. "If I could, I'd march right out of the world. But where would I go?"

Ereth continued on, grumbling and grunting, not caring where he was going, knowing only that he was heading into the deep woods, away from his home, away from everyone.

He reached a place where the trees grew so close even the air seemed to be made of shadows. He looked about.

Nothing moved. Nothing stirred. "I'm all alone," he whispered. "Utterly alone."

As he gazed forlornly about, he noticed a large boulder sticking out of the ground. One side of it glistened, sparkled almost. Curious, Ereth drew nearer and saw that embedded in the large stone was a piece of bright mica. He started to turn, only to catch a glimpse of his reflection there.

Ereth rarely looked at himself. It happened occasionally when he had to bend down to take a drink from a pond or stream. In those moments, he did not like what he saw and quickly shut his eyes.

This time he stared hard at the image of his face as if searching for something. "You," he said, "are *not* handsome. You are prickly! Ugly! Grumpy! Not friendly!"

He gulped down a rasping breath and then suddenly bellowed, "Erethizon Dorsatum, you are a self-centered and conceited porcupine! You should be ashamed of yourself, feeling angry because of Poppy. Think how she feels being dead!" Tears trickled down his blunt face.

He shifted his head in various directions, all but crossing his eyes to see himself. Then he moved his body around, trying to get a glimpse of his whole self. Finally, he pressed his nose flat against the mica, so that his eyes stared into their own reflection. "You," he said, as if addressing a stranger, "are a porcupine. An *old porcupine*. A *very* old porcupine. An antique porcupine. A prehistoric porcupine! A fossil porcupine. But what," he asked the image, "have you done with your long life?"

When no answer came from the stone, he supplied it himself. "Not much," he said.

"Have you done *anything* good?" he demanded. "Did you build anything? Solve any problem? Make anyone happy? Teach anyone anything?

"Erethizon Dorsatum!" he shouted. "You have done nothing with your life!"

He stood still, gazing at himself, panting with emotion.

"The only good thing you've done is love Poppy," he gasped. "And now that she's gone, what do you intend to do with what's left of this empty life of yours? Just tell me *that*, Mr. Ereth Dorsatum!

"You," he said, accusing his image, "were going to learn to . . . to . . . smile. Like Poppy always did. Fine! *That* will be your farewell gift to her. From now on you will . . . smile! Like Poppy!"

Ereth stepped back so he could see his whole face. "Did you hear me? Smile!" Peering at the mica, he tried to smile, but the creature that looked back at him only grinned hideously.

"You look like a belching bug," he cried. "You'll have to

do better than that!" He twitched his lips, first one way and then another. He pushed a paw into his mouth and pulled up one corner of his lips and then the other. Desperate, he snatched up a twig and stuck it in his mouth, pulled it out and up so as to create a smile.

"If Poppy were here," he cried, "she could have taught me to smile. She would have done it well, too! Well, I'm not budging until I teach myself!"

The porcupine stood in front of his reflection, struggling to smile. At last he sighed. "Smiling is too hard!" he yelled. "I should have started a long time ago."

CHAPTER 23

Bounder the Fox

POPPY CERTAINLY KNEW foxes ate mice. When she had met Bounder during her first visit to Dimwood Forest, he had tried to catch her but had succeeded only in chasing her into Ereth's smelly log. That was when she first met Ereth. The porcupine drove the fox away. She smiled at the thought. And here—after all that time—was the same fox! She wished Ereth were with her now. Her smile faded.

Poppy wondered if Bounder would remember her. Not that it mattered. If she was going to get out of the cave, she had to get past him.

She stayed where she was, occasionally peeking around the tunnel bend to study the fox. All the while Bounder remained asleep, barely stirring, taking deep, long, and sleepy breaths.

Poppy tried to recall what she knew about foxes' habits: they were fast, and clever, and did most of their hunting at night. That meant she would have to be very patient, and hope that when the day was over Bounder would get up and leave. Of course, this place could be his main den. Considering the bones, Poppy rather suspected it was. If he had just eaten—Poppy glanced at the bones again—and his belly was full, he might not venture away for *days.*

The warm air coming from the tunnel entryway told Poppy the heat wave had not broken. That could be another reason Bounder might stay put: the tunnel would be a lot cooler than out beneath the sun.

Waiting, Poppy ruefully recalled that a short while ago she wanted things to change. Now, here she was desiring nothing more than to return home and have things exactly as they were. *Be patient!* Poppy chided herself, even as she reminded herself that she had little choice.

Still, Poppy acknowledged that flying with Luci, seeing the bat cave, and meeting all those bats had been a wonderful experience. To pass the time, she mused about the possibility of another trip, going elsewhere, doing something completely new. Except next time—if there was a next time—she would take someone along, like Spruce.

The growling of her empty stomach interrupted her thoughts. Her anxiety returned. *Goodness,* she thought, *I never used to be impatient. I suppose I just want to make the most of the time I have.*

She peeked around the bend again at the curled-up fox. He was still asleep—or so it seemed.

Poppy studied Bounder's position. Though he was lying across the entryway—blocking it—she noticed that there was more open space in front of him than behind. Was that on purpose? Then she saw—not far from the fox's nose—a slab of rock leaning against the wall. Moreover, the rock's slant made a gap between the rock and the tunnel wall. That gap appeared just big enough for her to crawl behind. Poppy decided she could use the rock as a shield—if she could get behind it.

Without actually deciding to do so, Poppy knew she was getting ready to sneak past the fox.

Taking minute steps, Poppy slipped around the bend. Crouching very low, she crept along where the tunnel wall met the floor, inching forward in the direction of the entryway—and Bounder.

Every few steps she paused and studied the fox. The closer she came, the bigger he seemed. She glanced at the bone bits and shuddered. *Don't go any more!* an inner voice kept telling her. But another part told her she was safe because the fox was asleep and lay still except for the tip of his tail, which twitched ever so slightly.

She halted. *Was that tail telling her something? Was Bounder setting a trap? Was he just pretending to sleep?*

Poppy had to catch her breath. When the fox's tail stopped twitching, she inched forward, placing each foot slowly, deliberately down. She breathed as softly as possible. All the while she kept her eyes fixed on Bounder.

The fox's ears flicked. Poppy froze. She studied the leaning rock. And that gap. It was only a few feet away. Poppy decided it would be wise to rest behind the stone, in the gap, before making a final dash to the open air.

When the fox's movement ceased, Poppy continued on.

Bounder snorted. Again Poppy stopped. Her heart pounded. She held her breath. She was so close to the rock. When the fox's sounds subsided, Poppy edged forward again.

The leaning stone—and the protective gap—were no more than a foot away. Telling herself she *must* leap forward—*now*—Poppy tensed her leg muscles. She must not miss the gap!

At the last moment she darted a glance at Bounder. The fox's eyes were wide-open and he was staring right at her. He was grinning hideously, fangs exposed.

With a gasp, Poppy hurled herself toward the rock. She was not fast enough. Bounder slapped a paw down, blocking her way.

"Got you, mouse!" he bayed gleefully. "Got you at last!"

CHAPTER 24

On the Trail to Glitter Creek

SPRUCE GAZED down the trail. *I never thought Glitter Creek was so far*. All the same, he was positive, or mostly positive, that he was on the right path. And if it did lead to the creek and if he could find Grandma Poppy, it would be such a great thing. When he brought her home, he'd be a hero to everyone.

So Spruce pushed on, making frequent stops, sniffing the air, constantly shifting his ears. But the farther he went, the more he began to sense something odd in the air.

He stopped. Someone was coming along the path very quickly. Next moment a rabbit bounded up. Small and brown, the rabbit moved in jerks: three hops and a pause, three hops and a pause.

Spruce leaped to the side of the path to get out of his way. "Hey, Rabbit," he called. "Stop!"

The rabbit skidded to a halt and looked around. He used a paw to push a floppy ear away from his frightened eyes. "What?" he said. "What's that? Who called me?"

"It's me, Spruce. Is this the right path to Glitter Creek?"

The rabbit stared at Spruce. His nose twitched. He shoved his ear away from his eye again. "The creek?" said the rabbit. "Did you say creek? What creek?"

"Glitter Creek," repeated Spruce. "Am I on the right path?"

"The path?" echoed the rabbit. "To the creek? It certainly

is. But don't go there. You don't want to. Not at all!" With that he bounced away down the trail.

"Why?" Spruce called after him. "Why don't I want to?"

The rabbit stopped barely long enough to shout back, "Because it's bad. Very bad. As bad as it gets."

Spruce peered down the path and then turned back to the rabbit. "But . . . what's so bad?" he called.

The rabbit had gone.

Spruce shrugged, glad at least to know the path would take him to the creek. *That'll show Dogbane,* he thought with pleasure. *That'll show everybody!*

Confidence bolstered, Spruce moved along a little faster. What could be so bad?

CHAPTER 25

Poppy and Bounder

BOUNDER SHOVED HIS WET NOSE against Poppy's small, furry chest. His grinning lips curled back so that all of his sharp white teeth were visible. His breath, heavy with the stench of whatever animal he most recently had eaten, washed over her like a rancid rag.

Terrified, Poppy shrank back against the tunnel wall, her heart beating furiously.

"Well, now," said Bounder, "it's been quite a while since you and I have met, hasn't it?"

Poppy was too frightened to reply.

"Actually," the fox went on, "I've been watching you for some time. Ever since you stuck your cute pink nose 'round that bend in the tunnel. What were you doing back there? How'd you ever get past me to get in here?"

"I . . . I flew," Poppy stammered.

"*Flew?*" said the fox as he settled himself, while putting his other paw down. He now had a paw to either side of Poppy, trapping her.

"A bat brought me," said Poppy, struggling to keep herself calm. The more she and the fox talked, the better her chances were for escape.

"A bat?" said the fox. "Is that supposed to be a joke?"

"No, really, it's true," said Poppy, stealing looks about in search of some means of getting away.

Bounder grimaced. "Bats are horrid," he said.

"Actually," said Poppy, "I found them to be very pleasant."

"They seem to have caught you, didn't they?" said the fox.

"That's because a young one thought I was a moth," Poppy explained.

"A moth!" The fox laughed, again showing all his teeth.

"They only eat insects," Poppy explained.

"No worry about *me* confusing you with a moth," said Bounder. "I know you're a mouse, and I like eating mice. Small, but exceedingly tasty."

"I'm old and probably tough," said Poppy. If she could manage to leap over Bounder's front paw, and execute a really fast dash behind that slanting stone, she was convinced she had a chance to get away. That would require doing two things well: she'd have to take the fox by surprise,

and she'd have to quickly squeeze into that space between the wall and the rock—a tight fit.

"I suppose you might be old," Bounder said. "But I've no intention of making a complete meal of you. More like a between-the-meals snack." He lifted his right paw and held it as if he were about to smack it down on Poppy.

"Where was it we met before?" Poppy said in haste. "I'm

not even sure of your name." She knew the answers, of course, but asked in hopes the fox would talk some more—anything to give herself more time.

The fox lowered his paw. "I can't believe you've forgotten," he said. "My name is Bounder. Your name is Poppy. I met you a long time ago and gave chase. You managed to get away by running into a log."

"I was younger and faster then," said Poppy.

Bounder grinned. "We all were."

"But what caused you to so kindly let me go?" asked Poppy.

"Actually, there was an ugly porcupine in that log," said the fox with a frown. "You sure you don't remember any of this?"

"I'm sorry, Mr. Bounder, I don't," said Poppy. "But what happened? You know, when I ran into the log?"

"I really do have a good heart," said the fox, summoning what looked like a forced smile. "I decided to let you go. Anyway, I really don't like porcupines." His lips curled back in disgust. His pink tongue drooled.

"Is this your main den?" Poppy asked quickly. "It's quite nice."

"Too large for one fox," said Bounder.

"Then you live alone?" Poppy was calculating the length of the jump that would clear Bounder's paw and get her behind that rock.

"I'm afraid so," said Bounder. "I did have a wife. Good old vixen. Named Leaper. I'm sorry to say she died. Caught in a human's trap."

"How awful!" cried Poppy. All the while she watched the fox intently, knowing that she would have only one chance to escape.

"It was sad," agreed Bounder, not sounding very miserable. "But we all have to go sometime, don't we?" He grinned again.

"What about children?" Poppy asked. Sensing that Bounder was getting bored with the conversation, she knew she would have to make her move soon. "Do you have any?"

Bounder lowered his paw. "Three, actually. Grown up now. Moved away. Live in Dimwood Forest. A pretty ungrateful bunch, actually. I did a lot for them, but I don't see them much. I suppose that's what happens to every parent. How many children do you have?"

"Eleven," said Poppy. "Lots of grandchildren. Even great-grandchildren."

The fox shook his head. "All ignoring you, I suppose."

"Oh no, they're still very much around," said Poppy, gathering her strength in her rear legs. "We're quite close."

"What a nuisance," said Bounder. He began to open his

mouth wide in a great yawn. "I like children, but . . ." As he yawned, he involuntarily closed his eyes.

Poppy made her move. She leaped straight up in the air, twisted sharply about, and came down on the other side of Bounder's paw. No sooner did her toes touch the earth than she dived toward the leaning rock, squirming and kicking to get safely behind it.

Bounder, meanwhile, finished his yawn and opened his eyes. Poppy was no longer sitting between his paws. "Where the . . . !" he exclaimed, and looked around wildly, just in time to see her squirm behind the rock.

Down came his paw!

As Poppy squeezed under the cover of the rock, she felt Bounder's paw squash the tip of her tail. It took all her strength to yank it away—not without a little pain. Once free, she crouched down behind the rock, trembling.

She was safe—for the moment.

CHAPTER 26

Spruce Sees What's Bad

A CHEERFUL SPRUCE continued to amble along, reassured that he was truly heading toward Glitter Creek. Hadn't the rabbit said so? Besides, it felt good being out in the forest on his own. None of his brothers or sisters would have done so. Yes, the rabbit's warning puzzled him, but everybody knew rabbits were skittish. What could possibly be so bad? Well, yes, the heat was awful, but still. . . . *Maybe it's a fox,* thought Spruce. *Maybe it's an owl. Maybe it's a human. Maybe it's . . . nothing. Bet the rabbit was just being timid. Not like me,* Spruce told himself with pride.

A little farther on, the trees thinned enough so that Spruce could see a good deal of the sky. The more he saw of it, the hazier the sky appeared—rather like a fog. Was *that* what the rabbit was thinking of as bad: some *fog*? Spruce snorted with scorn.

But as the young mouse continued to stroll along the path, he became increasingly aware of a strange smell in the air. It tickled his nose. Made it itch. *What is that?* he wondered. Was *that* what the rabbit was referring to as something bad: a *stink*?

As Spruce pressed on, the strange smell grew stronger. His eyes began to smart. Then his throat became irritated. He coughed a few times.

There was a break in the trees just ahead. A tired Spruce hoped it would be the creek. When he got there, he would take a quick look about for Grandma Poppy. If he did not find her, he would go home.

A few minutes later, he stepped out of the woods and onto the bank of Glitter Creek. The path he'd been following had led him to the old wooden bridge that crossed the creek. On the Dimwood Forest side of the bridge—not far from where Spruce emerged from the forest—stood an old, dead, and charred tree. It looked as if it had been struck by lightning a long time ago.

As for the bridge, it was nothing more than decaying wooden planks placed side by side and thrown across the creek bed. But on the far side of the bridge—on a hill—was a steady boil of what looked like a cloud. But it was a cloud that puffed, billowed, and churned with fierce energy.

The cloud was quite dark in some spots. In other places

it was white. Swirling above it were big and small white specks, some that drifted up, while others floated aimlessly over the land. As Spruce gazed at it, he saw that within the cloud were red-and-gold bits, glowing and winking. He heard noises, too, snapping, crackling, and crinkling sounds, as well as a steady whoosh of wind.

The young mouse stood transfixed. He began to see red, orange, and blue fingers poking out of the cloud, as if pointing everywhere, trying to tear things apart. At the same time waves of heat washed over him, heat far greater than the summer's high temperatures. The heat seared his ears and nose, singed his whisker tips, and made his eyes blink and tear, forcing him to step back again and again.

What is this? Spruce wondered.

He began to remember talk from older mice, descriptions and hazy images of smoke, heat, and flames, all of it in tones that suggested something altogether dreadful, something they called *fire.* Gradually Spruce began to grasp that what he was seeing must be—had to be—that thing, that . . . *fire.*

Even after Spruce had named what lay before him, he continued to stare, terrified and fascinated at the same time.

As Spruce watched, the fire edged toward the far side of the wooden bridge. Bright sparks fell on the old planks.

The planks began to smolder, smoke, and then burst into flames. As the young mouse watched, the fire began to cross over the creek.

Suddenly Spruce understood: *That fire could catch me!*

Turning, he dashed back along the path toward home. He had not gone very far when he spied a hole partially hidden beneath a rock. He stopped, went to the hole, and sniffed to make sure no one was in it, that it was safe. He darted a look back. The fire was still there, advancing slowly. He dived down into the hole. Once inside, he turned around and peeked out, watching with a terrified fascination as the fire crept slowly in his direction.

CHAPTER 27

Poppy Tries to Escape

"YOU PESKY, sneaky mouse!" yelped Bounder, jumping up and shoving his paw behind the slanting rock as far as he could. "Trying to lull me with your friendly talk."

Poppy squirmed farther along the gap. Though it was impossible to stand, she managed to turn about to face the probing paw with its sharp claws.

Momentarily, the claw pulled back only to be replaced by the glaring brown eye of the fox. "You can't get away!" Bounder snarled. Next moment he withdrew his face and shoved his paw in again.

Poppy crawled toward the opposite end. But a narrowing of the gap and the roughness of the stone made movement difficult. Then, even as she approached the end, she saw the fox peering in at her from *that* side.

"Give up!" barked Bounder.

Poppy scampered back to the middle of the rock. Once there, she took a deep breath and tried to calm herself. Bounder was looking in from one side, leaping around, growling and yapping, then looking in from the other side. His barking boomed in Poppy's ears, deafening her.

"I'll just have to wait," Poppy said. She hugged herself and tried to push away all thoughts of hunger and thirst.

It did not take long before she became aware that the rock slab was shaking. She looked one way and then the other. At the end closest to the cave entrance and her path of escape, Bounder had wedged his paw deep into the gap. Though still safe from his grasp, it was perfectly clear to Poppy that the fox was trying to topple the slanting stone. If he succeeded, Poppy would be in the open. She would have no choice: She'd have to run for it. But which way?

The rock moved some more.

"Give up gracefully!" bayed the fox. "Accept your fate!"

Poppy made up her mind *not* to go back into the tunnel. *He'll only outrun me,* she thought. *Anyway, there's no real safety that way. My best chance—my only chance—is to get into the open. At least I'll have room to maneuver.*

Bounder snorted, snarled, and grunted. The rock shook and moved some more. *I'm going to have to run for it,* Poppy warned herself. She put herself in the best position. Then she had a new idea: *The last thing he'll expect is if I go directly at him. Right into his face. It's risky, but . . . Here's hoping . . ."*

Bounder had shifted the stone enough so that he was able to get his two front paws behind it. Then his nose. Poppy was sure it was only a matter of seconds before the rock flopped over. It was already beginning to totter.

She braced herself to leap.

With a final push, Bounder shoved the rock away from the wall. For a second it stood upright, teetering. Then it tumbled away from the wall, landing with a noisy clatter.

Completely exposed, Poppy leaped right at Bounder's face. Just as she was about to reach his nose, the fox jerked up one of his paws and batted her down to the ground.

Turning a somersault, Poppy came down hard. Stunned and groggy, she staggered up, knowing that she must run.

For a moment, Bounder was unsure where Poppy had landed and was still searching for her.

Poppy dived forward out of the cave's entrance, which opened to Dimwood Forest. *Run!* she told herself. *Run!*

But what Poppy saw next brought her to a complete standstill. She stood absolutely still, staring with horror. Smoke was rising from Bannock Hill. Amid the smoke were bright red flames.

"Fire!" cried a stunned Poppy. "Fire moving toward the forest!"

CHAPTER 28

The Bridge to Dimwood Forest

THE BRIDGE'S DECREPIT PLANKS, dried out by weeks of drought, burned very quickly. Within moments the entire bridge broke apart and fell, crashing down into the dry creek bed, sending up a cascade of orange sparks and flames that spewed in all directions.

Some of the sparks and flames landed on the nearby old dead tree. The ancient tree all but exploded into flames, burning like an angry, revengeful torch. It burned so fast it took only moments to topple, tumbling down into the denser forest.

And when it fell, Dimwood Forest began to burn.

CHAPTER 29

What Poppy and Bounder Did

POPPY, dumbfounded by the sight of fire, forgot about Bounder. Instead, she stared before her. Over Bannock Hill rose great plumes of boiling black-and-white smoke. Spikes of flame darted through the smoke like snake tongues. Trees were ablaze. Grass was burning furiously.

Abruptly, the fox's voice broke into her thoughts, even as his paw came down on her tail.

"You stupid mouse!" he barked. "You could have gotten away. But now—"

"Bounder!" cried Poppy, pointing. "Look! Over there!"

Bounder turned, looked, and gasped. "Good glory!" he cried, lifting his paw from Poppy's tail. "It's . . . it's . . . fire!"

Side by side, the two animals stared out.

"With the forest so dry . . ." Poppy's voice faltered.

". . . everything will be destroyed . . . ," Bounder continued.

". . . and everyone who lives there will be . . . ," Poppy went on.

". . . killed," concluded Bounder.

"Bounder," Poppy whispered, "my whole family is down there."

"My children are too," the fox replied.

"I have to warn them," said Poppy. "But . . . Bounder." She turned to look up at him. "I'll never be able to get there."

Bounder stared down at Poppy and then out again toward the fire. Next moment he lowered his head. "Grab hold of my ear!" he cried. "Pull yourself up. Quickly! We'll need to hurry!"

She looked up at him, not sure if she understood.

"Forget all that," Bounder growled. "This is different. Climb on or I'll leave you!"

Poppy glanced back at the fire, then turned back around and grabbed one of Bounder's ears, hauled herself up, and worked herself around to set herself just behind his head.

"Are you there?" said the fox. "You're so light I can't feel you."

"Here and ready!" Poppy exclaimed.

"Hold tight!" Bounder cried. "If you fall, I'll never know!"

"Go!" Poppy urged.

With Poppy clinging to his fur, Bounder plunged down

in a great leap, going so fast he all but tumbled down the ridge. Body low to the ground, bushy red tail streaming behind, neck stretched out, ears pushed back, the fox used his sharp nose to point the way. Charging forward with leaps and bounds over low spots, galloping furiously where it was flat, he raced as fast as he could.

Poppy, pressed between the fox's ears, tightly gripped tufts of his fur with her forepaws. The onrushing wind bent her whiskers back and flattened her ears. Every now and then she lifted her head and tried to see where they were. But the bushes, trees, and rocks flew by so quickly it was impossible for her to know, or even figure out, what direction they were traveling. It was terrifying. It was also exhilarating.

This is so much faster than flying with Luci, Poppy thought. *And much more dangerous!* She gripped the fox's fur even tighter.

Once, then twice, as Bounder made a sharp turn or took a jump and came down roughly, Poppy almost lost her grip. She had to force herself to concentrate on holding on. Then the fox took another soaring leap. He came down with such a rattling *thump,* the shock caused Poppy to lose her breath.

On and on they went until Bounder suddenly slid to a halt. His whole body trembling, he panted and took great gulps of air.

An equally breathless Poppy lifted her head and looked about. They were somewhere in the midst of Dimwood Forest. Thick, heavy smoke coursed in multiple layers, swirling now this way, now that. It stung her eyes and reached into her lungs, making her choke and cough. Its smell was a clotted stench of burning wood and leaves—sickening.

"Where are we?" Poppy called over the loud crackling

and snapping.

"Not . . . far from . . . the forest edge," the fox gasped as he tried to regain his breath. "Over there"—he pointed with his nose—"is the creek. Where do you want me to take you?"

"I need to get home."

"Which way is that?"

"Is that Glitter Creek ahead?"

"Yes."

"Do you know the bridge that crosses it?"

"Think so."

"If you can get me there," said Poppy, "there's a path that will take me home."

"Keep holding on!" cried the fox. Turning, he dashed toward the creek. Poppy put her head down.

It wasn't long before Bounder stopped again. "Poppy!" he called.

"What's the matter?"

"We're heading right toward the fire."

Poppy sat up and looked. The smoke was thicker, the stench stronger. Noises were louder, too. She could see flames. As awful as the summer's heat had been, the heat from the fire was twice as bad.

"How far to the creek?" she called.

"Just ahead."

"Hopefully the fire hasn't crossed over yet."

"Don't know. I'll try. Here we go. Hang on!"

As Bounder charged forward, Poppy dropped down again and gripped the fox's fur. The closer they came to the creek, the thicker the smoke, the louder the flames, the hotter the wind.

"Here's the creek!" cried the fox, coming to a skidding stop.

Poppy sat up. She had a fleeting impression that this was the spot where Ereth had almost drowned in the mud—where she had been flipped up in the air. But what commanded her attention now was the fire on the far side of the creek. There was smoke, thick black smoke. Even more appalling were the great sheets of flame that reached up like jagged red-and-yellow claws, ripping furiously at the sky.

"Poppy!" Bounder barked. "Look over there!" He pointed with his nose.

The swirling smoke made it hard to see anything clearly. But what Poppy did see squeezed her stomach: the old bridge, its planks engulfed in flames, had collapsed into the dry creek bed. The fire had spread into the forest.

Bushes were on fire. So were dry grasses. Entire trees were burning like towering torches. Other trees, glowing red orange, were tumbling and falling, spewing sparks in all directions, setting even more trees aflame.

"Bounder," she cried. "Can you see how far the fire has gone?"

The fox pranced up on his hind legs and then dropped down. "Can't tell," he said. "But it looks like the fire must have only just jumped the creek."

Poppy slid down his neck onto the ground. She looked across Glitter Creek, where the fire raged and roared.

Bannock Hill was no longer visible. She thought of the Gray House ruins—her old childhood home. She wondered what was happening there and, more importantly, whether her relations were safe. Then she reminded herself the house ruins were in the open. Surely the mice living there had seen the fire and escaped. Her thoughts turned back to her own family. If the entire dry forest caught fire . . .

"That's my path right over there," Poppy cried to Bounder. "I'm going home." She started off, only to stop and run back to the fox.

He looked at her quizzically. "What's the matter?"

"Thank you, Bounder!" Standing on her rear toes, she gave his sharp nose a hug.

Bounder stared after Poppy as she began to run down the path. Then he looked at the fire, which was now moving rapidly into the dry forest. "Poppy!" he barked. "Can you go faster than the fire?"

She paused. "I'll run."

"It's burning too fast," said the fox. "The heat is too great. Let me take you."

"Bounder! You've got your own family to find."

"I don't even know where to start looking," barked the fox. "Come on! Get back on."

Poppy hesitated.

Bounder leaped to where Poppy was. "Hurry!" he barked, pawing the ground with impatience.

"Bounder . . ."

"Do it!" he all but snarled, shoving his nose into hers.

Poppy took a leap, landed on the bridge of Bounder's nose, and then ran up his face to where she'd been before, between his ears. This time, however, she stayed high, wanting to be able to direct the fox.

"Holding on?" called Bounder.

"Yes!"

"Straight down that path?"

"Unless I tell you otherwise!"

"Here we go!" the fox bayed, and started forward with a trot, only to shift into a gallop as he skirted close to the fire, close enough so that his hair singed.

Poppy, clinging to the fox, heard the fire's roaring, crackling ferocity and could feel terrible heat on her back. She felt compelled to look and was all but blinded by the intensity of the flames when she did.

"Am I going right?" barked Bounder.

Poppy swung around and shouted, "Yes!" But even as she turned she lost her grip. The next moment she tumbled to the ground, striking her head.

Bounder, unaware that Poppy was no longer with him, raced on.

Poppy lay still on the ground in the middle of the path. Behind her, the fire continued to spread.

CHAPTER 30

Where Is Spruce?

Ereth had informed Junior about the dell that he had selected for Poppy's funeral service. Junior, agreeing, said, "There will be at least a hundred of Poppy's closest and dearest relations. The ones who loved her most. Children, grandchildren, great-grandchildren. Which is to say, everyone."

Ereth, thinking *I loved her most,* smiled.

"And Uncle Ereth," Junior reminded the porcupine, "you will make just a *few* opening remarks, won't you? The rest of the family, my brothers and sisters, want to speak."

Ereth continued to smile.

Junior considered him with some puzzlement. "Uncle Ereth, are you all right?"

"Of course I am!" cried the porcupine. "Why are you asking?"

"Because you are, well, smiling. And you never smile. It looks . . . somewhat . . . odd."

"I don't care what it looks like. I am smiling because I want to!" Ereth snarled through his smile.

"But this is such a sad time. Why are you smiling . . . now?"

"If I want to be sad by smiling, then I'll smile!" shouted Ereth. And he put his paws into his mouth and pulled the corners of his lips to either side so as to make the widest grin possible.

Junior considered the porcupine. "And, I just realized, you're not swearing either."

"Listen here, you pickled—"

"Pickled what?"

Ereth smiled broadly. "Never mind."

"Fine with me," said Junior, shaking his head. "We'll have the service today, at twilight. It should be a little cooler by then."

He turned away but glanced back.

Ereth leaned forward and grinned at him.

When Junior returned home, he told Laurel about the arrangements Ereth had made for the service later that day.

After listening, Laurel said, "Junior, do you have any idea where Spruce is? I haven't seen him for quite a while."

Laurel and Junior asked their children if any of them knew where Spruce had gone.

Clover said, "He went to find Grandma Poppy."

"Poppy!" said Junior. "Why would he do that?"

"He said she went flying somewhere."

Junior sighed. "Did he say where he was going to look?"

"Glitter Creek."

"Are you sure?"

Dogbane said, "I was going with him, but then I decided to come home. He kept going."

Junior conferred with Laurel. "Glitter Creek is a long way off," he said to Laurel. "I'm not even sure he's been there before."

"Now, Junior, you know how often Spruce has taken off on his own. I wish his brothers and sisters were as independent. And he always gets back safely, doesn't he?"

"But Poppy's funeral service is going to start soon. He doesn't know anything about it."

"We'll leave Dogbane here," suggested a calm Laurel. "When Spruce returns, the two of them can come along to the dell together. Now, I think you'd best consider what you're going to say at the funeral, and don't worry about Spruce."

CHAPTER 31

The Rescue

IT WAS A VERY FRIGHTENED SPRUCE who crouched in the hole beneath a rock, wishing someone were with him, wishing he were home, wishing he had never come. Every few moments he crept to the mouth of the hole and peeked out. All he could be sure of was that the smoke was getting thicker.

Maybe, he considered, *it would be better if I went down deeper.* But even as he began to retreat, he heard the sound of galloping pass by, followed by a soft *plop!*

Then—silence.

Spruce was afraid to move. *It's some animal,* he thought. *A big animal. It was running. I bet it was running from the fire. The way the rabbit was running. Maybe I shouldn't be hiding, just running.*

He listened hard, straining to hear if the animal was still there.

Hearing nothing, Spruce crawled to the top of the hole and carefully peeked out. Though there was a lot of smoke, he saw nothing of the fire. But he did hear crackling, which told him the fire was close. Then he noticed something on the path. He stared at it. It was a mouse.

Next moment Spruce's heart seemed to turn over. "It's Grandma Poppy!" he shouted. "She's landed!" And he leaped out of the hole and ran to her side.

"Grandma Poppy?" he cried, leaning over her. "Are you all right? What was flying like?"

When she did not reply, the terrified mouse looked toward the creek. He saw flames coming toward him. They were spreading quickly in all directions—including his—snapping and snarling like the angriest of animals.

"Grandma!" cried Spruce. "You have to get up!"

Poppy stirred and blinked open her eyes. "Spruce!" she cried. "What are you doing here?"

"I came looking for you," said the young mouse.

"Thank you. But why?"

"Uncle Ereth said you flew away. Did you?"

"In a way, yes." Poppy sat up and looked around. "Where's Bounder?"

"Who?"

"The fox who was taking me to warn the family about the fire."

"A fox?" cried Spruce. "Oh wow! Do you have a friend who is a fox?"

"I suppose you might say so. I fell off. He must not have noticed." She considered Spruce. "I'm glad he didn't."

Poppy stood up, gave herself a shake, and then looked in the direction of the fire. The flames were much closer. "Spruce!" she said. "We need to get home fast. To warn the family."

"I know. But, Grandma, I did find you, didn't I?"

"You certainly did," said Poppy, with another look

at the fire. "Now let's run."

"Okay."

They ran down the path at full speed. When they paused to catch their breaths, Spruce asked, "How did you learn to fly?"

"Actually it wasn't me who did the flying, but a bat."

"A bat!" cried Spruce, his eyes very big. "Do you have a bat friend, too?"

Instead of answering, Poppy looked to see how far the fire had reached. For the moment they were safe, but she was quite sure their time was short.

"Would they take me flying, too?" Spruce asked.

"I'm sure they will. Now, less talk. We need to go very fast!"

It was Ereth's log that they reached first. Poppy turned to Spruce. "Run home to your father and mother," she said. "Tell them about the fire. I'll be right there."

The young mouse raced away, calling, "Dad! Mom! Everybody! I found Grandma! I really did! She really was flying. With her bat friend! I'm going to fly, too."

Poppy, meanwhile, plunged into Ereth's log. "Ereth!" she called. "Are you in here? You need to get out!"

When no reply came, she ran inside, only to discover that the log was deserted. She dashed out and saw Spruce running toward her. Dogbane was with him. When

Dogbane saw Poppy, he stopped.

"There's no one home," cried Spruce. "Except Dogbane with a message for me."

"What's the message?" asked Poppy.

Dogbane, still staring at Poppy, said, "Everybody's gone to the dell."

"Who is everybody?"

"The whole family."

"Why are they doing that?" asked Poppy.

"It's . . . well . . . ," stammered Dogbane. "It's . . . your funeral."

Poppy stood speechless.

Spruce tugged on her. "Grandma," he said, "if it's your funeral, aren't you supposed to be there?"

CHAPTER 32

Poppy's Funeral

ERETH WAS THE FIRST to arrive at the site of Poppy's funeral. "I'm the mourner in chief," he muttered. "I *should* be the first one." He was determined not to budge from his speaking post. No mouse would take his place! Front paws folded under his chest, he gazed at nothing and practiced his smile.

The sky turned quite hazy until it became so overcast Ereth was sure it was going to rain. Except there was not the slightest scent of rain in the air. On the contrary, it felt drier and hotter than it had all summer. The porcupine lifted his nose and sniffed. There was a strange smell in the air, but nothing he could place.

The day's light was beginning to fade when Junior, along with his brothers and sisters—Mariposa, Snowberry, Walnut, Columbine, Sassafras, Crab Grass, Pipsissewa,

Verbena, Scrub Oak, and Locust—and their spouses, and all their children, and their children's children made their way into the dell. As they came, Ereth stared straight ahead, with only an occasional twitch of his tail and a curt nod to the few mice he knew by name. To all he offered what he considered his best smile.

The mice who knew Ereth kept looking at him. He could hear them twitter: "What's Ereth smiling about?" "It can't be a smile." "Ereth never smiles."

The younger mice stared up at Ereth, too, speaking to one another in whispered undertones.

"There's the great Ereth."

"Wow! Poppy's best friend!"

"If he was Poppy's best friend, and this is her funeral, how come he's smiling like that?"

"Maybe he's going to throw up."

"Hey, guess what? Have you heard? Spruce is missing."

Ereth heard these words, but he remained quite still and continued to smile.

Junior climbed onto the rock and whispered into Ereth's ear, "Uncle Ereth, I think everyone is here. We should begin."

"Fine," replied Ereth, smiling.

"Uncle Ereth," Junior whispered, "you haven't seen Spruce around, have you?"

"No."

"I'm afraid he's wandered off. One of his brothers said he went looking for Poppy."

"He'll never find her," said Ereth, smiling broader.

"Well, you better begin," said Junior. "Better keep it to a few remarks, okay? I'll speak next. Then some of my brothers and sisters want to speak. But Uncle Ereth?"

"What?"

"Really, why are you smiling?"

"Want to."

"It's . . . well . . . strange."

"Beat it!" snarled the grinning porcupine, and Junior stepped away from the stone, but, along with his siblings, stayed close.

Ereth sat up. "Okay," he shouted, loud enough for all in the dell to hear. "It's time we began."

Almost two hundred mice stopped their conversations and stared up at Ereth, their ears cocked forward, with an

occasional twitch of a tail.

"My name," began the porcupine, "is Ereth. I suppose you know that. You should know it. If you don't, I'd have to ask why you haven't been paying attention. Anyway, this is all about . . . Poppy. We all know . . . knew . . . Poppy. But no one knew her better than me, since—"

When Ereth paused to catch his breath, Laurel whispered to Junior, "That's not a very nice thing to say."

"The point is," Ereth went on, "Junior asked me to make a few remarks. I suppose I could give a brief summary of Poppy's life. All about her parents,

Lungwort and Sweet Cecily. Where she was raised, Gray House. I could mention Ragweed, too. Briefly.

"I don't know why, but Poppy always thought Ragweed was something special. Not that *I* ever met him. Wish I had. I'd have given him a quill up the snoot."

Pipsissewa turned to Verbena. "That's so rude!"

Ereth continued. "That Ragweed, he was always mixed up in things. Even after he died. Don't exactly know how. Or why. But he was." Ereth shook his head.

"Or," he continued, "I suppose I could tell you about Poppy and that owl, Mr. Ocax. Of course, if she hadn't met *me*, things would have been very different. Because it was with one of *my* quills and *my* advice that she defeated him."

"I thought this was going to be short," Laurel said into Junior's ear.

"So naturally," Ereth went on, "you'll want to know how she met *me,* how *I* was able to encourage her, give her a sense of the real world, get her to grow up."

Ereth put his paws into his mouth and grinned while gazing down at the puzzled eyes of the mice.

"Let me see if I can get him to stop," said Junior. He began to move forward.

Ereth, seeing Junior coming toward him, hurried on. "But then I could explain how Poppy asked *me* to go with her on a trip to tell Ragweed's parents how Ragweed died. Naturally, *I* went. And that's how, because of that trip, of which *I* was in charge, she met Rye. Fell in love with him. Married him. Not that *I* understood why. I could mention Rye's poetry. But I don't want to because I couldn't stand it."

Junior was now close to Ereth. "Uncle Ereth . . . ," he whispered.

"Buzz off, fur ball," muttered Ereth, and went on. "I could tell you," he said, louder than before, "in case you never heard it, about the great battle with the beavers. If it hadn't been for *me,* all of Ragweed's family—Rye's family—would have been beaten up. Fortunately *I was* there. Gave those beavers a few pokes. That battle made it possible for Poppy and Rye to stay together. Me, again."

"Ereth . . . ," Junior said. "I really think that's enough."

Ereth shoved Junior back and boomed on. "Anyway, since *I* was so important in all of those happenings, the hero, actually, I could talk about that, too. For instance, Poppy and Rye had children. Too many, if you want to know what I think. Fact is, Poppy and Rye were too young to be parents. Fortunately, *I* lived close. They used to come and ask me for advice about how to raise you annoying kids. *I* gave them plenty. In fact, I could give a brief talk about how to be a good parent. Might be useful."

Ereth sighed deeply, caught himself, and grinned.

"Uncle Ereth," said Junior, standing right next to him, "you really need to—"

"Just getting to the really important part," Ereth muttered under his breath, and kept on. "So it would be only right to explain how she felt about *me*! After all, we were the best of friends. *Best,* best friends. Which means I should give a little talk about . . . myself. *My* early life. How *I* came to Dimwood Forest. Naturally I'd include how *I* met Poppy. I was saving her from a fox. I could even talk about that fox's children. *I* took care of them too. *I* saved them from starvation. That's me, always helping someone."

"Ereth, please. . ."

"And speaking of starvation, I suppose I might explain how *I* see life here in Dimwood Forest, what we could do once this heat wave passes—"

"Ereth! Stop!" shouted Junior.

"I suppose that's enough," said Ereth. "For introductory remarks. Of course, if there's time, someone else could speak. But they had better keep it short and only about Poppy. Long, self-centered speeches are stupid.

Besides, the whole point is, Poppy has gone and died!"

"But that's not true," cried a voice from the back of the dell. "I'm right here!"

CHAPTER 33

Poppy Alive

All the mice swung around to see who had called. There, at the back of the dell, stood Poppy. By her side was Spruce.

There was a great gasp of shock and surprise.

Ereth leaned forward and, seeing Poppy, bellowed: "Poppy! You suffocating sack of squirrel spit! Is that you or your ghost?"

"Why . . . it's me, of course," returned Poppy. "Who else would I be?"

"But I saw your ghost vanish into the sky!" yelled Ereth. "You're supposed to be dead!"

"Dead? Ghost? Ereth, I've never heard anything so silly. Look at me, for goodness' sakes! I'm very much alive."

"Then you're fake alive!" screamed Ereth. "And that's worse than being dead."

By this time Junior had found his voice and was able to say, "But Mom . . . never mind Ereth. Where were you? What happened?"

"Junior, please tell me what's going on here."

"Uncle Ereth told us that he saw your ghost flying up in the air."

"Well, though I did go up into the sky, I certainly am not a ghost."

"Dad!" shouted Spruce. "It was bats who taught Grandma to fly!"

"Junior," said Poppy, "aren't you pleased that I'm alive?"

"Yes, of course!" cried Junior. "Very happy. Aren't we?" he said to the crowd.

"Yes!" "Of course!" "Absolutely!"

"And I'm so glad that Spruce is with you," said Laurel.

"Spruce," said Junior, "we were getting worried. Where did you go?"

"I had to find where Grandma landed after her flying."

"And did you?"

"As a matter of fact," said Poppy, "he did. But never mind me. Do you have any idea what's happening?"

"What's happening, baboon bottom brain," shrieked Ereth, "is that we're in the middle of your funeral. In fact, I just gave a beautiful speech about you. I even learned to smile because you died. What a waste! Let me tell you right now, I've no intention of ever smiling again! Not even when I die!"

"But if we don't hurry," cried Poppy, "we *will* be dead. All of us. The forest is on fire!"

"Fire!" someone shouted.

"Did she say fire?" called another.

"What fire?" "Where's the fire?" "I don't see any fire!"

Spruce, standing next to Poppy, yelled, "Everybody! Listen to Grandma! The forest is really burning! I saw it! Listen to Grandma. She always knows what to do."

"Truly?" came the frightened voices of the mice. "Honestly?" "Not a joke?" "First she says she isn't dead." "Then she said *we* will be dead." "I don't get it." "What's happening?"

"There is a fire," cried Poppy over the chatter. "And every minute we stand here it's getting closer."

The mice began to scream, shout, and cry.

"Where do we go?"

"What do we do?"

"What about my home?"

"We're doomed!"

"We'll be killed!"

"Let me out of here!"

"Not that way!"

"This way."

"Which way should we run?"

"Somebody, help!"

"Help!"

Junior leaped up on the boulder. Standing next to Ereth, he called across the teaming dell, "Mom! Poppy! Where's the fire coming from?"

"From Bannock Hill," Poppy called back over the frightened, jabbering mice. "It's leaped Glitter Creek and is coming this way. Spreading quickly in all directions."

Ereth, who had been staring at Poppy with a mixture of fury and disbelief, looked up. He could now see that the sky was full of billowing, churning dark smoke. When he looked in the direction of the creek, he saw spikes of flame cutting through the trees.

"Thundering turtle toilets!" he cried. "Poppy's right! Look! The whole forest is on fire!"

Now the sounds of burning were unmistakable: the snapping, crackling, and crashing of falling trees seemed to come from every which way.

"How do we get away?"

"Can we escape?"

"Should we go now?"

"Should we stay?"

Poppy, standing as tall as she could, called to her children across the dell: "Mariposa! Snowberry! Walnut! Columbine!

Sassafras! Crab Grass! Pipsissewa! Verbena! Scrub Oak! Locust! Junior! Each of you. Head off in different directions. Find where the fire has reached, where it's heading! Then get right back here and tell us. See if there's a way out."

Poppy's children scattered. When they had gone, Poppy made her way through the crowd, reassuring now one mouse, now another, telling each one to keep calm, that they would all surely find a way to escape. Spruce stayed by her side. Reaching the other end of the dell, Poppy climbed up on the rock where Ereth was still sitting.

"Ereth," she said, "I'm so glad to see you!" She reached up and kissed his nose.

"Glad!" he cried, rubbing the kiss away. "I want to know where you went! Here I've been—"

"Ereth," said Poppy, "we'll talk later. We've got to deal with the fire."

"Mom!" came a call from across the dell. Scrub Oak had returned from scouting. "The fire is only about a hundred yards that way," he yelled, pointing.

The next moment Pipsissewa appeared, coming in from another direction. "The fire is over there!" she called.

One by one, Poppy's children returned. Each had the same message: the fire had spread all around them. They were surrounded.

CHAPTER 34

Surrounded

POPPY STOOD ON THE ROCK beside Ereth. All the mice were staring at her, as if she would know what to do, as if she would know some way of escape.

She gazed around. Through the ring of trees surrounding the dell she saw flames leaping and darting, moving about like mad dancers to the sounds of the all-consuming fire and roaring wind. Within the dell the air was growing thicker and heavier with smoke. The heat was almost unbearable.

"Grandma Poppy!" cried Spruce. He had been telling his brothers and sisters about his adventures, but seeing Poppy on the rock, he ran over to her.

"Spruce, I'm trying to decide what we can do—"

"I thought of what to do," Spruce shouted to her. "Call

your bat friends. Get them to fly us all out of here."

Poppy stared at Spruce. Then she said, "Spruce, that's a wonderful idea. Brilliant!"

"Everybody," she cried out. "Listen to me! There is a way to get out of here. We all need to call."

"Call whom?" cried someone.

"A friend of mine," replied Poppy. "Luci."

"Luci?"

"Who's Luci?"

"What's this Luci going to do?"

"Never mind Luci! We've got to get out of here."

"No, no!" shouted Poppy over the increasing din. "It's the only way. It's Spruce's clever idea. But we have to do it all together. As loud and as high as we can, shout—Lu-ci!"

Lifting her head, Poppy began to shout in her loudest voice, "Lu-ci! Lu-ci!"

Spruce was the next to take up the call. "Lu-ci! Lu-ci!" he called.

Junior joined in, followed by Laurel and all their children. Next were the rest of Poppy's children and their children—until all the mice in the dell were crying, "Lu-ci! Lu-ci! Lu-ci!"

Again and again they called, while the sky grew darker and the fire crept closer.

As Poppy cried "Lu-ci! Lu-ci!" she kept her gaze aloft, staring into the ever-thickening smoke.

A shrill, squeaky voice came from above: "Miss Poppy! What's happening?" The young bat swooped in and landed on the rock right next to Poppy. "Told you I'd come if you called. But oh my gosh! This fire is awful!"

"It's a bat!" cried one of the mice, and backed away. "It'll kill us!"

"Kill it first!"

"No, no!" shouted Poppy. "The bat's our friend."

"They'll teach us to fly," cried Spruce.

Poppy turned to Luci. "Luci," she pleaded. "Please, we need your help. Fly back to your cave—fast as you can. Get as many of your family as possible and bring them here. You've got to fly us out of this place."

Luci looked at Poppy and then at the mice in the dell. "Really?"

"Absolutely," said Poppy.

"Miss Poppy," said Luci, "there's fire all over Dimwood Forest. It's getting hard to fly."

"Please," Poppy pleaded. "It's the only way to save us. Please, just try!"

"I'll be back as soon as I can!" cried Luci, and off she flew.

As soon as the bat was gone, Poppy went to the edge of the rock. "Everyone!" she called. "Listen to me. The bats are my friends. They will be yours, too. I'm sure they will come. When they do, don't be frightened. They can carry us to safety."

"They'll teach us to fly!" shouted Spruce again.

"When they come," Poppy continued, "they'll be able to pick you up by your backs. It won't hurt, I promise. I've already done it. It's the only way we're going to get out of here alive!"

The mice stared at her.

Poppy felt a nudge from behind. It was Ereth.

"What about me?" he whispered in a frightened voice.

"You can come, too."

"But . . . but they won't be able to pick me up by my back."

Poppy stared at him for a moment, then said, "Ereth, it'll have to be your belly. It has no quills. It's soft."

"My . . . *belly*?" he roared.

"Ereth, it's the only way."

"Pickled pink pockets!" cried Ereth, backing away. "I can't. I won't. It's not right. It's humiliating. It's my one tender spot. Everyone will laugh at me."

"They won't!"

"Will!"

"Ereth, listen to me. I've been to the bat cave. Have you any idea what's there?"

"I don't care!"

"You do!"

"Don't!"

"It's *salt*!" she cried.

Ereth stopped moving away. He peered at Poppy

through the thickening gloom. "Did you say . . . salt?"

"Yes! Right there, in the bat cave. I've never seen so much. A whole beach of soft salt."

Ereth stared at her. He began to salivate. "A whole . . . beach . . . of . . . salt?"

"Enough for the rest of your life!"

"The bats!" came a cry. "They're back. Look at them!"

Poppy looked up. Down through the clouds of swirling hot smoke fluttered hundreds of bats into the dell. Their wings beat the air, pushing the smoke away.

"We're here! We've come!" their voices cried, high and shrill.

"Lie down!" Poppy shouted to the mice. "Quickly! Let them grab you by your backs! Hurry!"

It was hard to know who squeaked more, the bats or the mice. But as the bats hovered over the dell, dipping and diving, Poppy could see one mouse after another lifted away. Most were carried the way she had been, by the back. In two instances she saw small great-grandchildren carried by their tails. And at one point she was sure she heard Spruce shout, "Hey! I'm flying! Like Grandma!"

"Miss Poppy," Luci called, "what about this huge, prickly mouse?"

Poppy turned. There was Ereth. He was alternately

cowering in the midst of some two dozen bats, then spinning and smacking about with his tail. The bats kept approaching the porcupine, only to leap away when he lashed out.

"Ereth!" cried Poppy. "Stop! Be calm! Just roll over. It's the only way they can pick you up."

"Toenail toothpaste!" bellowed the porcupine. "It's insulting! Humiliating!"

"*Salt,* Ereth," cried Poppy. "Think about that salt! Salt enough for the rest of your life!"

Ereth blinked at Poppy. Then, drooling a little and muttering, "Salt! Salt for the rest of my life. Salt for the rest of my life!" he rolled over and stuck his four feet straight up in the air. Bats instantly clustered over his belly. Poppy saw Ereth rising—upside down—in the air.

"Great gobs of chicken cheese!" Ereth bellowed as he disappeared up into the smoke. "This tickles!"

"That's everybody but you, Miss Poppy," Poppy heard Luci say into her ear.

Poppy took one more look around the dell. She was indeed the last one. The flames had crept in very close and had reached the base of the boulder. The howl of burning filled her ears. Each second the air grew hotter, scorching hot, so hot her whiskers curled. Even as she gazed about, the trees surrounding the dell exploded into flames.

She looked at Luci, nodded, and then offered her back.

The young bat sprang over her and gripped her fur. "Ready, moth-mouse?"

"Ready as I'll ever be," said Poppy.

Luci unfolded her leathery wings, flapped them furiously, and soared up in a tight spiral.

Poppy, eyes closed, felt the terrible heat and the buffeting winds. She smelled the acrid stench of burning. Then the heat and the stench retreated, though her eyes still smarted from the dense smoke. At last, when fresher winds blew into her face, Poppy opened her eyes, looked down, and gasped.

All of Dimwood Forest was burning. Flames lit the sky, reaching enormous heights as if trying to pull it down. Black, gray, and white smoke billowed and roiled. Patches of smoldering scarlet dotted the earth like a glowing crazy quilt. "It will all . . . all of it . . . be gone," Poppy whispered.

Then she looked ahead and saw the swarm of bats carrying her family to safety. Amid them she could see the bulging bulk that was Ereth. And she was almost certain she could hear him bellowing, "Bring me to the salt!"

When Poppy looked down again, her tears—tears of sadness, tears of relief—fell. Whether they reached the burning forest she never knew.

CHAPTER 35

The End

FOR FIVE DAYS the fire raged, roared, and ravaged Dimwood Forest, and then gradually died away.

On the sixth day curls of smoke continued to trickle upward like whispered memories, while the charred trees stood like tall, crooked skeletons. Nothing moved. The earth was burnt over black. The land was silent and hot. Dimwood Forest was no more.

On the seventh day rain began to fall. It fell softly, as if the sky were kissing the earth.

CHAPTER 36

The Beginning

IT TOOK A FULL MONTH for the smoldering ground that had been Dimwood Forest to cool. Gradually, the mice began to emerge from the bat cave. Though there were those who went elsewhere, some made their way back to the places they had once lived. Slowly, their lives resumed.

Among those who returned to the forest area were Poppy and her immediate family. And Ereth.

The old porcupine was pleased that Poppy had not died, pleased that he did not have to smile anymore, pleased that he was free to swear again, pleased to know where he had a life's supply of salt.

One day Poppy was sitting on a rock surveying the fire's destruction when Bounder appeared quite suddenly and sat down before her. "Glad to see you're okay," he said.

"You too," returned Poppy. "Bounder, I can't thank you

enough. That was quite a ride."

"It sure was," said the fox.

"Were your children all right?" asked Poppy.

"Sure. A little singed, but fine. Yours?"

"Very much so. Thanks to you, everyone was saved."

"Glad to hear it." Bounder stood up. "Hey, mouse," he said with a toothy grin, "I'll catch you next time." He turned and trotted away. Just before he took a bend in the path, he looked back, winked, wagged his tail, and then went on.

Poppy never saw Bounder again.

* * *

It was a week later, twilight. The air was sweet and dew laden. The sun, setting in the west, filled the cloud-laced sky with strokes of purple and orange. Poppy and Ereth sat atop Bannock Hill. Spruce was with them. For a long while they sat in silence. Then suddenly Poppy cried, "Ereth, Spruce, look over there!"

Spruce looked where Poppy pointed, but the porcupine only muttered, "Toasted tiddlywinks on toast. I don't feel like looking at anything."

"No, really, Ereth. You *must* look," insisted Poppy, and she scampered a few feet. "Please come over here!" Spruce joined her.

With a loud grunt, Ereth heaved himself up and waddled reluctantly to where Poppy was peering down at the ground. "What is it?" he demanded.

"Just look!" she insisted.

Ereth and Spruce stared where Poppy was pointing. A tiny green shoot no more than an inch high had pushed up through the blackened earth.

"Things are starting to grow again," cried Poppy.

"Does that mean the whole forest will come back?" asked Spruce.

"I think so," said Poppy.

"So what?" muttered Ereth. "You won't be here."

"Ereth," said Poppy, "how many times do I have to tell you? I need to go to another place for a while. I want to see what else there is in the world before I get too old. And Spruce said he would come with me."

"Why Spruce?" demanded Ereth.

"'A mouse has to do what a mouse has to do,'" Spruce said.

"That's not you talking, that's Ragweed," Ereth grumbled. "Always Ragweed."

"Grandma says you should come too," said Spruce.

Ereth turned to Poppy. "Why can't you stay here?" he demanded.

"Because when I visited the bat cave I learned that there's a whole lot beyond Dimwood Forest. I want to see even more."

"How are you going to do that?"

"Ereth," returned Poppy, "with the forest gone, the bats can't find enough insects to live on. They've found a new home in an old mine in another forest some miles from here. I'm going with them."

"You're not a bat," said Ereth.

"I like bats," said Spruce. "They're fun. Luci takes me flying all the time. We're best friends. We're going to have adventures."

"Ereth," said Poppy, "it's like what Oldwing said. As long as you try, you're young. Now, it's twilight. Luci will be here in a few moments to take me. I wish you would come with us."

"Uncle Ereth, the bats offered to take you too," said Spruce.

Ereth shook his head. "I'll never fly again."

"Walk, then," said Poppy. "I've told you how to get there. It's not that far. Go straight north."

"I'm too old to move," Ereth objected. "Anyway, there's all that salt you found for me. I'd be a fool to leave that."

"Then, Ereth, at least promise me that you'll visit."

"Greedy green geese! I'm not promising anything to anyone."

"Then, my dear, dear friend, we have to say good-bye."

"I said good-bye to you once," cried Ereth. "I don't intend to say it again!"

"Then . . . what else can we say?" asked Poppy, her eyes filling with tears.

"Nothing!" snapped Ereth. "Just go. Forget about me. I'll forget you, too. Have yourself a grand old time. So will I."

Poppy peered up into Ereth's face. "Oh, Ereth, I do love you," she said. "You really have been the best of friends. Thank you for always being you."

"Just go!" shouted the porcupine.

Even as they stared at each other, Luci and another bat arrived in a flutter of wings.

"Miss Poppy!" cried Luci. "Spruce! We're here. Are you ready?"

"Almost," said Poppy. She stood up on her rear toes and gave Ereth a kiss on the tip of his nose. "Good-bye, my dear, dear friend," she said. "I will always miss you!"

"Go away!" yelled Ereth, and he turned his prickly back on her.

"I will," said Poppy. To Luci she said, "I'm ready."

"Bye, Mr. Ereth," called Luci. "If you change your mind, you can come too. We'll take you." She giggled. "Belly up!"

"Never!" growled Ereth.

Poppy lay down. Luci hovered over her, gripped her back as gently as she could, and lifted her in the air. The other bat did the same to Spruce.

"Good-bye, Ereth," Poppy called down as she and Luci circled upward. "Good-bye!"

"Good-bye, Uncle Ereth!" called Spruce.

And off they flew.

Ereth turned and stared after Poppy, watching as she headed north, then disappeared into the sky. The old porcupine shifted about and gazed in the direction of the bat cave, where all that salt was waiting for him—enough salt for the rest of his life. Ten lives.

He shut his eyes and lifted a paw to touch the tip of his nose.

Suddenly Ereth opened his eyes and bellowed, "Baggy buffalo boxers! Poppy! Spruce! You tiny tuffs of tinsel wits! Wait! I've changed my mind. I'm coming too!"

And the porcupine began to run in a northerly direction.

CHAPTER 37

Rye's Poem

ICE LEAF

A green summer leaf
Embraced by the frozen ice
Keeps memories warm